Not Yet Summer

To Reese,
Enjoy!
Susan Brown

Not Yet Summer

by

Susan Brown

Yellow Farmhouse Publications

Not Yet Summer
ISBN Print Edition: 978-1544984223
ISBN eBook Edition: 978-1544984227

Copyright © Susan Brown 1980 and 2017
Scholastic-TAB Publications Ltd.
123 Newkirk Rd., Richmond Hill, Canada 1978
ISBN 0-590-71025-7

Revised edition
Yellow Farmhouse Publications, Lake Stevens, WA, USA
Copyright © 2017
Publication Date: April 2017

Excerpt from *Sammy and the Devil Dog*
© 2017 by Susan Brown
Excerpt from *Hey, Chicken Man!*
© 1978 and 2017 by Susan Brown

Cover and Interior Design: Heather McIntyre
Cover&Layout, www.coverandlayout.com

Cover Photography: Girl © Cheryl Casey; Factory © L.F

For all my girls and

All my boys

Forever

Other books by Susan Brown you might enjoy

Hey Chicken Man
Something's Fishy at Ash Lake,
An Amber & Elliot Mystery written with Anne Stephenson

Susan Brown's fantasy books!

Dragons of Frost and Fire
Dragons of Desert and Dust

Coming soon!

Sammy and the Devil Dog	*April 2017*
Catching Toads	*September 2017*
You're Dead, David Borelli	*2018*
Pirates, Prowlers and Cherry Pie	*2018*
Twelve, *a mythic fantasy*	*2018*

As Stephanie Browning, written with Anne Stephenson

Outbid by the Star	
Undone by the Boss	
Balancing the Books	*2017*

Not Yet Summer

Contents

Prologue

For almost seven years the warehouse had been empty. Once the town had made a profit leasing it to a succession of companies, but now it was too small for modern business needs, and so it stood abandoned and unnoticed among the squat, grey buildings that lined the cemented-up banks of the town's dying stream. As winter turned to summer and then to winter again, the building became rundown, its windows broken, the locks on the doors smashed. There was no money available either to tear down or to modernize the warehouse; so it stood as it was, empty, except for occasional strays that took refuge before looking elsewhere for a home.

2   Susan Brown

Chapter One

Marylee

When the alarm clock went off, Marylee slapped it with her hand, then lay back, trying to recapture the haven of sleep. There had been a dream – a rare thing of happiness and warmth. It lingered in her consciousness like beads of sunlight strung out in a haze, warming and drawing her. If she could just sleep awhile longer....

"Marylee!" Mrs. Watson rapped sharply on the door to her bedroom. "Get up. I heard that alarm, so there's no use pretending you didn't. You'd better not be late for school again!"

Marylee heard her walking briskly down the hall and pictured her squat form, her small-featured face. Her foster mother's face was routinely kind, but somehow it never warmed to affection.

Reluctantly Marylee opened her eyes. She stared at the blue wall with the framed magazine picture of a boy hauling in a fish from a foaming stream.

It was one of the two things in the room she really cared for – in spite of the grinning boy. The rest of the room was like the intent of the picture – square, dull and boyish. The Watsons had always had boys as foster children before, and the room was still impersonally geared to the male gender. The only concession to her sex was the bouquet of artificial flowers hastily stuck in one corner.

Except for the boy's intrusion into the scene, the picture evoked a wild freedom that Marylee longed for. There were old trees, some bent, some upright, all crowding down to the stream. The water gurgled and rushed over the rocks, foaming around the jagged edges. Way off in the background were mountains, misty blue and solitary.

Once, between foster homes, Marylee had been sent to a camp in country like that – a magic time. Her raging soul had emptied into the laughing water, and the twisting hurt and loneliness had drifted away into a haze. The silent trees had crowded close, feeling warm and loving when she stretched her childish arms around them. She had never cared for the lifelessness of her doll after that – after she had hugged the cool, living warmth of the great trees.

And the counselor had not told Marylee she was odd when she had whispered that she imagined the trees as people who would love her and sweep down their leaves to hug her. The gentle woman had smiled, and three days later had given her a book about four children who had found a country where trees walked and animals talked. She still had the book, ragged now from her love of it, carefully placed in the locked box where she kept her few treasures.

But the camp had been almost six years ago, when she was only eight – when her short, weak leg had simply made her feel miserably different from the other people who drifted into and out of her life. She had been too young then to realize that her lameness was a curse, the reason she was always alone, always alone and hated.

"Marylee!" Mrs. Watson called sharply. "For heaven's sake, are you going to get up?"

Marylee's lips pursed as familiar hatred drove the old memories away. Resentfully she pulled herself up and finally lurched out of bed. She was hungry. Might as well get up and eat.

But first she paused to examine the pale green flower shoots in the plastic pot balanced on the narrow window ledge. Marylee had filled the pot with earth from the garden as soon as the ground had thawed, almost a month ago. Before long the small shoots would bud and then flower.

A slight smile, stiff because it so rarely appeared, hovered on her lips. She loved small, growing things, things she could care for and make blossom. Once someone had said that she had "a way" with her. Marylee still cherished that stray compliment.

The kitchen smelled good when she finally limped downstairs. Pancakes and sausages, she noted with a tinge of pleasure. Mrs. Watson was a good cook, and as people went, she wasn't too bad. She talked too much about Marylee's limp, but at least she didn't look away or drip sickening pity over her, as most people did.

Once Marylee had thought the people cared and had been merely embarrassed by their reactions. But as little incident had piled on little incident over the years, her naive hopes about people had been worn away, leaving only a cynical hatred of them all.

"Good morning," Mrs. Watson said, too brightly.

Marylee sat down wordlessly and helped herself from the heaped plates on the table.

"There's something I have to talk to you about, dear," Mrs. Watson began after an uncomfortable pause.

Marylee looked up at her for a moment and clenched her jaw slightly. She hated that false word, "dear." When people called her that, they never meant it.

Nervously Mrs. Watson wiped her hands on a towel.

"Mr. Watson and I have talked about this a lot lately, so I don't want you to think it's a hasty decision. Or a personal one either," she added, with an embarrassed titter that was foreign to her normal manner. "But we feel we're really too old to continue parenting as we have in the past. We want to live our lives more for our own enjoyment now – travel a bit, get prepared for our retirement. So I'm afraid we'll have to give you up. We've already told Mrs. Wojansky of our decision, and the Children's Aid are trying hard to find a new home for you. I hope you understand our position, dear...."

There was a long, cold pause as, fork suspended halfway to her mouth, Marylee stared at her foster mother.

"Yeah, sure. Why not?" she said loudly, indifferently.

Deliberately she resumed eating, trying to ignore the sick feeling of fear churning in her stomach. Another home – another set of people to discover how much they really didn't like her.

I hate them. I hate them.... The words ground through her mind. But she had to seem normal. She had to go upstairs, brush her teeth, collect her books and sweater.

She found herself counting everything – the number of times the toothbrush slid over her teeth, the number of steps she took to cross the hall and enter her room, the number of papers she flipped through to find her homework page.

One, two, three, four, five... one, two, three... one... one...

Fiercely she bit her lip and forced her mind away from the monotonous drone of the number counting – her instinctive refuge from the searing hurt that was boiling up in her throat.

Oh, how she hated them....

"Time to go to school," Mrs. Watson called up the stairs. "Don't forget to take a sweater. It's not summer yet."

Numbly Marylee picked up her sweater and backpack and left for school.

The spring sun shone at an angle through the broken window of the warehouse, making Marylee's shadow strangely long and distorted on the debris-strewn floor. She didn't notice, however. Her eyes were shut, her body hugged to herself as she tried to raise memories of that beautiful warm forest and stream.

Aspens shiver, red maples wave,
While I and my enemies lie
Still
In the grave.

She shivered with melancholy pleasure at the poem she had made up. But she would have to go soon. They would all be looking for her.

"So who cares!" she whispered, tossing her head so the straight strands of brown hair slid over her shoulders for a moment before they drooped back around her face. She hugged herself tighter, relishing the feelings of hate that had soared through her that morning at school.

The sun, unusually hot and bright for the last day of March, was beating down on the asphalt of the school yard. Marylee leaned back against the wall of the school so that the shadows shrouded her slightly.

A group of girls had organized a game of skipping. Normally they would have felt themselves too mature to indulge in such a childish game, but the sunshine and the fresh air had raised their spirits. A hint of wistfulness grew in Marylee's mind as she watched them. Angela had a new outfit – another of the many things her parents showered on her curly blonde head. She was in the center of the girls now, laughing merrily.

As usual, they ignored Marylee.

She wondered what it would be like to be included in everything the gang did. Well, maybe she'd give it a try. A week or two more – a month at the most – and she'd be gone anyway.

She pulled herself upright and stared at the other girls. Taking a deep breath, she limped toward them, chin lifted. In a moment Marylee stood beside her giggling classmates, waiting stiffly for someone to acknowledge her presence. No one said anything.

"I want to play," she announced loudly.

The other girls looked at her in embarrassment. One of the gushy ones regarded Marylee's leg with obvious pity. "Do you think you should?"

"I want to play!" Marylee repeated in staccato tones.

"You can't just barge in where you haven't been invited. Jeez, are you rude!" Angela remarked, placing her hands on her hips and glaring at Marylee.

"It's a free country," Marylee said defiantly, breathlessly. "If I want to play, I can."

There was a cold pause. Miserably, Marylee realized she had done it all wrong – but there was no way to back down or to smooth over her presence.

"All right, if you want to play," Angela snapped, "then play!" She threw one end of the long skipping rope to another girl, so that Marylee was in the center. Then she began turning the rope.

Desperately Marylee hopped, trying to keep her balance despite her bad leg. Once, twice she managed to jump the rope. But Angela twisted it faster and faster and the rope began slapping Marylee's ankles as it turned first one way and then another.

"You wanted to play," Angela taunted. "Well, play then!"

Marylee stood still, frozen, as the rope snapped painfully across her skin. The circle of giggling girls closed in on her, snickering louder and louder. Marylee's hate churned up, pounded in her head, and finally broke loose.

She grabbed the swinging rope, jerking it out of the girls' hands. Then she shoved Angela, hard. Angela staggered slightly and Marylee pounced on her, pushing and shoving, finally tripping her.

"I'll show you!" Marylee shouted wildly, bouncing heavily onto Angela's stomach. "Have some dirt! It suits you!"

Gleefully she rubbed handfuls of dirt and gravel into Angela's clothes, all the while jabbing at her with her knees.

"Stop it! Stop it!" Angela shrieked. Her eyes were streaming with tears. The other girls stood in a circle, openmouthed and unmoving.

"Bitch! Bitch! Bitch!" Marylee screamed in glorious, roaring hate.

Then suddenly she felt someone pulling on her arms. The roaring died slightly. A teacher yanked Marylee roughly to her feet.

"What's going on here?" she demanded furiously, shaking Marylee's arm. "Who started this?"

"Marylee did!"

"Marylee started it! She shoved Angela down!" "She called her a bitch!"

"She rubbed dirt all over Angela and we couldn't stop her!"

"Marylee!"

The sun was low now, the shadows almost melted. Marylee's shorter, weaker leg had begun to feel numb. Cautiously she flexed her toes, waiting for the pins-and-needles feeling of returning circulation.

I'll take another look at my garden, she told herself. No way she would run home for them.

The garden was a patch of sandy soil where the concrete had broken up. Marylee had spent long, painful hours carrying the heavy chunks of cement to where she could dump them into the sluggish green water of the stream. Her limp had become worse from the strain.

But she had a garden all her own. No one else knew the feel of that coarse sand-dirt, or the rich smell of good peat moss and fertilizer worked into the soil. In her mind she could smell and feel every particle of the ground she was making come alive. Soon there would be flowers – something beautiful left behind even after they sent her to a new foster home.

Well, she could spend lots of time nursing the ragged patch of earth now – the principal had suspended her. There was a lot of talk which had floated by her exhausted indifference. Telephone calls, too. Everyone was informed – Mrs. Wojansky, her case manager, and the Watsons, her soon-not-to-be foster parents.

There were many solemn words, heavy pauses, and meaningful noises from the principal's mouth. Marylee paid no attention;

it didn't matter. Then he told her to go get her things and wait on the bench in the outer office.

She just shrugged at him and tried to saunter casually out of the office. But instead, she limped, her weak leg making the harsh *shuuing* sound she hated. She limped down the empty halls, hearing lonely echoes of other kids in their classes. Once she had retrieved her backpack and sweater, she had slipped out a back entrance and walked to the warehouse – her warehouse. No one knew she came here.

"Who would care anyhow?" she muttered defiantly as she limped across the floor toward the small window. Who cares about *anything*, she thought as she put her head out the square, glassless hole. She folded her elbows on the sill, peered down at the worked soil of her garden below and then out at the smelly stream only a few yards away.

Maybe once you were a real brook, she thought, not all poisoned and crippled by the cement. A real brook....

A shrill bark pierced the quiet. A dog! A dog had trotted up and was digging at her garden, ripping out her seeds!

"Stop! Get away!" Marylee shrieked. She beat her arms, trying desperately to slap the dog away. But the window was too high.

Frantically, she looked around for help. A boy with a lean face and uncombed hair was standing a short distance away, grinning and sipping on a carton of milk.

"Stop him! Please!" she pleaded.

But he just shrugged and stood by indifferently while the dog tore into her seeds.

Susan Brown

Chapter Two

Petey

"Petey!" his mother called.

Camper pricked up his ears, and his tail would have begun thumping on the blankets if Petey hadn't grabbed it and held it still.

"Quiet!" he hissed, shutting his eyes so he would look as though he were still sleeping. Camper gazed at him quizzically for a moment, then laid his grizzled muzzle down on the pillow, his nose nestled under his master's chin. They had slept this way for almost eleven years – since Camper was a puppy and Petey just toddling.

"Petey," his mother called cheerfully as she banged into his room, "you'd better get up or you'll be late for school."

Petey stayed still. No way he was going to roll over and yawn and listen to her cheerful lies.

"I know you're awake!" There was growing exasperation in her voice. Petey's hands and teeth clenched angrily.

"Get out of here!" he snapped suddenly, rolling over to glare at her. Camper jumped slightly and whimpered. Petey slid his hand under the dog's head and rubbed his silky throat.

"Don't use that tone of voice with me," his mother said uncertainly, pausing awkwardly in the middle of the room. "I'm your mother and I deserve some respect!"

"Who says?" Petey snarled. "Why should I respect you? You don't even tell me the damn truth!" He was close to crying, knew it, and hated his mother for making him feel that way.

"What are you talking about?" she said, avoiding his eyes. "When did I lie to you?"

"Last night!" Petey muttered, his voice breaking painfully. "You said you were working an extra shift, but I called you. You didn't pick up because you weren't there! You were over with Mike again. You lied to me!" His voice rose into a hoarse half scream.

"Don't get so upset." His mother tried to laugh but her voice sounded unusually breathless. "So what's wrong with me spending some time with one of my friends on my night off? It's pretty rough, you know, working all night when other people get to be at home and live a normal life."

"But what about me!" Petey cried hoarsely. "Why can't you be at home with me for once? You don't care that I'm all alone here! You like that stupid Mike more than me. So why don't you just take off like Dad did and get it over with!"

"Shut up!" his mother shouted. "Just shut up! I take one free night to spend with a friend and you carry on as though I was an irresponsible bum like your father. You've got Camper to look after you! Who have I got to look after me? No one! So I find someone who does care about me and it's a big crime to spend some time with him!"

"Yeah, but what about me!" Petey cried fiercely. "*Me!* I'm not like Dad. I'm not a no good bum who's going to run out and leave you when you need help. Why do you have to go and leave me on your night off! Why don't you ever want to be with me!"

"Stop screaming at me! You're just like your father – yelling about nothing!"

"I'm not!" Petey shouted.

"Yes, you are!"

His mother paused, sighed, and wearily rubbed her fingers through her short blonde hair. She took a few steps toward him.

"Try to understand, Petey," she said more quietly. "It isn't that I love Mike more than you or anything. You're my kid and that makes you special to me. But you're still a kid and sometimes I've just got to talk to an adult. What if I tell you about how hard it is to buy the things we need on my lousy salary – "

"I listen," Petey protested.

"Sure you listen," his mother said with a half smile, "and you try hard because you're a good kid. But that's not your kind of worry yet, and you won't really be able to understand until you've lived through that particular kind of hell yourself. So I talk to Mike about it – that and other things – and it makes me feel like a person again. I need to feel like a person too, sometimes," she said intensely.

She looked ready to cry and Petey felt glad about it, glad he had hurt her the way she hurt him. How could she say he was like his father? He wasn't! He'd never take off like that no-good bum. Never!

"I'm going to school," he said shortly, getting out of bed and heading for the bathroom.

As he dressed he could smell bacon frying – a peace offering from his mother. Bacon was reserved for special mornings.

Wordlessly Petey went into the kitchen, took a piece of toast, piled bacon on it, folded it into a sandwich, and walked out the door with Camper padding along behind him. He pretended he didn't notice his mother standing helplessly in the middle of the kitchen, a spatula dangling loosely in one hand and tears trickling through the night-before's makeup on her cheeks.

For an hour he wandered – hating his mother, feeling torn and aching inside. Eventually he reached his school, and almost as an afterthought remembered that today was a school day.

"Stay," he told Camper. The dog sprawled out in the spring sun and panted affably at his master. Petey ran up the steps, through the door and down the hall to his classroom.

"Peter! What do you mean by coming in at this time of the morning?" His teacher glared at him. The hate for his mother transferred to this other woman who didn't understand how he felt.

Petey lounged into his seat and fixed his eyes on her coldly.

"Oh, I didn't have anything else to do, so I thought I'd come by and make your day." His mouth smiled as the class tittered, but his eyes remained hard and his nostrils flared slightly.

"I've had enough of your insolence." The teacher's voice rose slightly. Petey only shrugged. "All right," she ordered, "down to the office."

Petey felt a cold knot in his stomach, but he made a point of taking his time to get up. The principal had told him the last time that he'd better not get into trouble again.

"So what can he do," Petey muttered to himself as he walked down the hall.

The secretary told him to wait on the bench outside the office. It seemed a long wait, a long time to keep up the bravado.

Finally the office door opened and a girl with a bad limp came out. Petey knew that she was in a grade higher than he was, that the kids teased her all the time. As she passed by, she looked at him without seeming to see anything.

"All right, Peter," the principal said. Petey forgot all about the girl with the limp.

Petey sat on the cemented up bank of the stream, swishing a stick through the water and occasionally sipping on a large carton of milk – the remains of the late lunch he had bought for himself. Camper lay quietly beside him, enjoying the warm spring sun.

Petey hadn't been long in the principal's office. It was the horribly cold, efficient kind of session that reduced him to mute fear. He was suspended from school. If there was any more trouble when he came back, Jackson told him, he would be expelled for good.

Although after the phone call to his mother, he was ordered to go home, Petey went wandering instead, finally ending up by the stream. He would have to go home eventually, but maybe if he waited long enough his mom would have gone to work. Or to Mike's, he thought bitterly.

She kept saying he was getting to be like his father. But he couldn't be like him. His dad had run out on them. And Mom hated his father.... He couldn't be like his father.

He threw the stick into the stream and stood up.

"C'mon, Camper," he said, aimlessly heading toward the line of factories and warehouses a little way away. Sometimes there was interesting debris left around that he could cart off. Camper trotted ahead and began scratching vigorously in a patch of dirt beside an abandoned warehouse.

He heard a shriek.

Hanging out of the warehouse window was the girl he had seen limping out of the principal's office that morning. She was shouting at Camper and flapping her arms wildly – a comic strip scene so silly he forgot his misery and grinned.

"Stop him!" the girl shrieked.

Petey shrugged.

"Stop him! Please!"

"He won't hurt you," Petey snapped scornfully.

"I'm not afraid of him, you idiot!" she screamed back. "I've planted a garden there!"

"So okay!" Petey grumbled. "C'mere, Camper."

Camper looked up reluctantly, then trotted over to Petey's side and sat down. Petey pulled out a candy to reward his obedience.

The girl disappeared from the window. In a moment she reappeared around the side of the warehouse and glared fiercely at Petey. She knelt down in the dirt to cover the seeds again.

"When did you plant them?" Petey asked unconcernedly.

"Day before yesterday," the girl mumbled. "If they don't come up, you'll sure be sorry."

"Yeah, sure! You and how many others!" Petey mocked.

The girl stood up suddenly, her shoulders rigid and trembling.

"You shut up!" she shouted, jumping him. They went down in a flailing heap, Petey caught unawares. Suddenly Marylee screamed. Camper's muzzle was clamped around her skinny arm.

Petey rolled out from under her. "Let go, Camper!" he ordered. The dog released Marylee's arm.

"Are you some kind of lunatic, jumping me like that?" Petey demanded angrily. "My dog might have killed you!"

"Some chance!" she said scornfully. Camper whimpered as Petey rubbed his ears. "Is he okay?" Marylee asked.

"What do you mean, is he okay? You're the one he bit! You think he's going to catch rabies from you or something?"

"No, I don't," Marylee said stiffly. "He didn't even break the skin on my wrist – he just held me. But I kicked him with my shoe. It's a special shoe and it's heavy."

"Hey, Camper," Petey said quickly. "You okay, boy? Do you hurt anywhere?" Gently he felt around the dog's body. Camper winced slightly when the boy touched his left shoulder.

"Should we take him to a vet?" Marylee asked anxiously.

"Maybe. Try walking, Camper."

With Petey's coaxing, the dog walked around, but stiffly. Gradually he began trotting normally.

"I guess he's okay." Petey sat back on his heels and eyed her narrowly.

"Um – I'm Marylee Jones," Marylee said. "Who are you?"

"Petey – Petey Davies," he replied. "What the heck did you jump me for?"

"Well, so what if I did?" Marylee said, suddenly angry again. "You all think you're so perfect just because you don't limp, and I'm sick of it. Any more dumb cracks about my leg and you'll be sorry!"

"Hold it, will you? I didn't say *anything* about your cruddy leg," Petey snapped. "Boy! I've heard about you at school. No wonder no one can stand you!"

"Oh, yeah?" Marylee retorted, hoping desperately she wouldn't cry. "Well, one more word and I'll give you some real trouble."

Petey looked at her in disgust. "Yeah, sure," he muttered.

They were silent as Petey crouched, rubbing Camper's muzzle. "Anything in that old place?" he asked finally, gesturing toward the warehouse.

Marylee toyed with the idea of ignoring him or hitting him. "No, not much," she said finally, uncertainly. "Some old boxes, an office with the windows smashed, a couple of broken chairs – that kind of garbage."

"I'll take a look at it," Petey said. He stood up and started around the corner of the building.

"What are you, the building inspector or something?" Marylee called sarcastically. He didn't answer, so she limped after him. He had squeezed through the broken side door and was casually rummaging among the scattered heaps of broken boxes.

"What are you doing?" Marylee asked.

"Looking, just looking. There's always things to find. Not here, though," he muttered after a minute. His eyes strayed back to her. "How come you aren't in school?" he demanded.

"I was suspended for beating up a kid who made a crack about my leg," Marylee said with a toss of her head.

"I've been suspended. Big deal, isn't it?"

"Yeah," Marylee answered with a stiff half-smile. "It's just awful the way they've given us a vacation . I don't know if I can stand it!"

They looked each other over for a moment, then wordlessly wandered outside. They walked along the bank of the stream, past a dozen squat warehouses, a few sagging abandoned buildings, and a long row of factories. They said nothing. They were both too absorbed in their own thoughts to bother talking.

"Don't people get mad when you take things you find around here?" Marylee asked idly after a long while.

"No. Most of it has been thrown out. People don't lose this stuff – they just pitch it out."

Petey stopped to watch Camper. "Hey, there's something over there."

Camper was sniffing it – a large, battered duffle bag leaning in the shadow of a factory. "What did you find, boy?" Petey called casually.

They heard a crackling sound as the dog scratched against the side. Then there was another noise – a long, thin wail.

"There's something in there!" Petey yelled excitedly.

Marylee didn't answer. From the endless rounds of foster homes she knew that sound.

How she knew! Then she was running hard – shuffling and limping and tripping – to the bag, to that cry, her heart pounding and freezing in her stomach.

"Oh, my God," she whispered hoarsely. "Oh, my God, my God."

The bag reeked of the sour smell of vomit and urine. Inside, the baby tried to open her swollen eyes, thrashing her arms and legs weakly.

Gently Marylee picked the child up and clutched her close, rocking back and forth on her heels, making little hushing noises. The child reached up her arms and clasped them around Marylee's neck, burying her head under Marylee's chin and whimpering in miserable exhaustion.

As Marylee held her, the baby relaxed slightly. After a few moments her breathing became even and she fell asleep, her hands still clutching the warm collar of Marylee's shirt. Marylee held her in motionless, warm silence.

"How did a baby get in there?" Petey finally asked in a bewildered voice. "People don't leave babies in duffle bags. I mean they don't carry them in bags and just forget them by a factory...."

Marylee hardly heard him. She held her breath.

She must not scream. She must not allow this relived horror to well up from her stomach. She had to forget that this was how she imagined her own mother abandoning her – carelessly dumped for anyone to find. Not wanted. Thrown away.

Carefully, she let out her breath, then took another deep one. A loud noise would waken the baby. The baby must be protected. She was too little. Too small.

"They leave babies in bags, or boxes, or anything at all if they're abandoning them," she said slowly, desperately keeping her voice at an even monotone. "Abandoning them...."

She lowered her head and pressed her lips against the soft down of the baby's head. When she was a baby had anyone ever held her so, felt soft baby hair against the lips? Maybe the faceless person who had accepted her from the faceless mother.

"How can somebody just leave a baby?" Petey broke into her abstraction. "I've never heard of anything so weird."

"Weird! It's not weird. It happens all the time," Marylee said. "Who ever wanted me? I'm lame, so they didn't want me. People don't want other people who aren't perfect."

"But there's nothing wrong with this baby," Petey insisted, unsurely. He felt stupid and frightened, not knowing what to do but sure there was something terribly wrong. "People don't just leave babies," he repeated. Even when they'd rather not bother, like his mother, he thought suddenly. "We'd better get the police or something," he said finally.

"No!" Marylee hissed. "No! *I* found her! She's mine! No one else wanted her. You said people don't lose things they want – they threw her away! I won't let them pass her around because no one wants her. I won't let them make her like me. 1 want her! She's mine! I'm keeping her!"

"But you can't!" Petey argued. "You can't look after a baby! You're too young. What are you going to do? Take it home and say 'Look what I found! Is it okay if I keep it in a drawer of my dresser?'"

"I don't care," Marylee said grimly, turning so that her body was between Petey and the baby. "I'm not too young. I'm fourteen. And it doesn't matter anyway because I'm keeping her. I'll find a way to look after her. No one else wants her, so she's mine. She's mine and I will love her." She took a deep breath. "She'll never, ever think someone doesn't love her."

Suddenly Marylee looked up, her face white and hard.

"Will you help me? A baby needs a father as well as a mother."

"But I'm only twelve! I can't!" Petey said quickly, feeling as though the world had suddenly gone spinning crazily around him:

"If you can't take it, if you want her left like garbage, then take off!" Marylee snarled. "I'll do it myself. Just don't you dare tell anyone. Boy, you'll sure be a no-good father for some poor kid!"

"But we can't do it!" Petey cried desperately. "I'm not a father. I'm only twelve! We can't look after a baby by ourselves. Where would we keep her? How would we feed her?"

"Lots of kids just a bit older than us are married and have a baby. They do it somehow." Her face was set with determination. "I'll do it.

I'll do it by myself if I have to, so take off! You're nothing but a no-good bum! You'd probably take off on us anyhow, just because it isn't all easy. Go on! Get out! Go away!" Marylee was almost screaming. The baby woke and began her pitiful wailing again.

"I'm not!" Petey shouted back. "I'm not a no-good bum like my father! I wouldn't run out like him...." But his words were drowned out by the growing momentum of the baby's cries.

The two children stood helplessly, trying to gather themselves, as the cold springtime sun beat down on the bleak concrete and steel of the factories. The baby continued to cry miserably.

"Maybe she's hungry," Petey said after a moment. He remembered the half-full carton of milk he was carrying. He held it out to Marylee. She snatched it. "It should be a bottle," she muttered.

"Try the straw."

"Here, baby darling. Try this," Marylee cooed, gently pushing the straw into the baby's mouth. In her hunger the baby began sucking hard, first gasping on the air, then choking as the milk rushed into her mouth.

"She doesn't know how to drink like this. We've got to have a bottle."

"We can get one later," Petey said uncertainly. The baby choked again.

"It's not working," Marylee cried frantically. "She keeps choking. Maybe she can drink – "

She pulled the straw out of the carton and quickly hoisted the baby to a sitting position. Then carefully, gently, she tilted the carton so that the milk trickled into the baby's mouth a few drops at a time. The baby spluttered and wailed weakly, but slowly, dribble by dribble, Marylee emptied the milk from the carton into the child's mouth. The last little bit trickled out and down her chin. Finally the baby lay cozily against Marylee once again, still clutching the collar of her shirt, and fell soundly asleep.

Marylee felt a rising lump in her throat as she cuddled the baby to her, feeling the helpless heaviness of her as she slept.

"What do we do now?" Petey whispered.

Marylee looked up reluctantly. "I don't know," she said quietly. "But we'll manage somehow."

34   Susan Brown

Chapter Three

April

The sounds in the warehouse were hollow, falling abruptly into the still, dusty air. Warily Marylee peered into the dim recesses of the building, watching for the scurrying sounds to turn into mice or rats that might threaten her baby.

"Poor baby," she murmured, pressing her lips to the sleeping infant's head. "Poor little April. But don't worry, you're safe now. Petey's gone for the things you need and I'm holding you close to me. I'm going to call you April because tomorrow is the first day of April. Tomorrow is the first whole day of our lives together, little baby darling. I'm going to be such a good mother to you. We'll love each other so much, every day. And I'll never leave you where no one wants you. Never, never, never."

Mice forgotten in the strange bliss that was stealing over her, Marylee slowly surveyed the warehouse, imagining how it would be when she had a chance to fix it up for her baby.

Those old boxes would be converted into a cradle and a little dresser. The office, once all the broken glass was swept out, would be her baby's bedroom. It would be safe from draughts. She would bring her small pot of flower shoots to stand on the dresser. Tomorrow she would buy some fabric – maybe pink gingham – to line the cradle and cover the dresser. She would sew little ruffles on them. Her baby would be surrounded with ruffles and cuddling and lullabies and love.

Lullabies and love....

The shadows had almost disappeared in the creeping dark by the time Petey came back. Marylee's arms were beginning to ache from holding the sleeping baby.

"Did you buy everything I told you to get?" she whispered.

"Yeah. I think so," Petey answered. He proudly placed two paper bags on the dusty floor before he dropped down beside her.

"I didn't have quite enough money but I talked the guy in the store into letting me have everything anyhow. There's diapers, things to wash her bum with, a bottle, milk, baby cereal, five jars of baby food and a plastic spoon. Pretty good, huh?"

"Yeah," Marylee answered wearily. "Will you hold her for a minute? My arms are so tired I think they'll break."

"What if I drop her?"

"You'd better not!"

She limped across to the window that overlooked her garden and stared, unseeing, at the stream that crept between the concrete banks. Far off to the right, the red rim of the sun slid behind the uneven silhouette of the rooftops of the city.

Suddenly she turned to Petey and tossed her head so the thin strands of hair hung behind her shoulders for a minute.

"How much change was there?" she asked.

He looked up in indignant surprise.

"None. I told you before, I didn't even have enough for this stuff, but I talked the guy into letting me – "

"How are we going to buy more?" Marylee demanded.

"What do you mean, more?" Petey suddenly looked frightened. "This will do for now, won't it? I mean, how much do babies eat? And you'll give her up in a couple of days anyway. I mean, you've got to!"

"I don't have to!" Marylee said fiercely.

"And I won't! She's mine, I tell you! And I won't ever give her up. She's yours now, too. You're her father."

Petey looked down at the baby. His baby, she said. He ached to scream that he didn't want to be a father, that it was too much for him, that he was going to run away. But then he would be a no good bum – like his father. No! His mother hated his father.

There was a heavy silence, a long, stretching, aching silence in the warehouse. The baby stirred slightly in Petey's arms and rubbed her tiny face closer to his shoulder. He felt her warm aliveness.

"Okay," he said finally. "I'll get some more money somehow."

Marylee smiled slightly and limped back to him. Petey felt warm and good inside – and scared. So very scared.

It was completely dark by the time Marylee limped up the sagging steps of the Watsons' front porch. Her stomach ached with hunger – she hadn't eaten since morning – but she was humming to herself

"It's terrible what goes on in the world these days." Mrs. Watson's voice came floating through the screen door. "What kind of person would kidnap someone...."

The light in the living room streamed across the dark hall and through the square screen, making the rooms inside look like a shadow box. Marylee could see the Watsons sitting on the sofa, apparently watching television. She could hear the smooth voice of the announcer.

She stopped on the porch and looked in.

Any other night she would have slammed in defiantly, demanding her supper, shrugging indifferent shoulders to the scolding that would come. It had never mattered.

But tonight it mattered. They would want to know where she had been, what she had been doing. Maybe they would make her stay in for a few days as punishment. She could always defy them, slip out when they weren't looking. But then they would call the Child Services and complain about how difficult she was. Marylee knew the whole routine – it had happened to her many times before with other foster parents. In the end there was always a quick move to a new place – another treatment center or a new foster home.

Before, it hadn't mattered. Now it did.

April needed her. If they moved her, Petey would get frightened and turn April over to the uncaring faces. She would never see April again. Nothing mattered now except April.

Marylee took a deep breath and slowly pulled open the door.

As though their heads were operated by the same string, the Watsons turned to look at her.

"Well," Mrs. Watson said, her voice icy with irritation, "nice of you to drop by."

She stood up and switched off the television. Marylee bit her lip fiercely. She must not tell the old witch off. She had to keep control, for April.

"Sorry," she muttered. "I – I didn't realize it was so late. I – "

"It was getting dark, wasn't it? Don't you think you've caused enough trouble for one day?" Mrs. Watson's voice was harsh as her pent-up annoyance spilled out.

"Go easy on the girl, Linda," Mr. Watson interrupted. "I daresay she hasn't had a very good day. You needed some time to think things out, didn't you, Marylee, after the trouble at school?"

Marylee had forgotten about being suspended. It was of no importance, but she seized on it as the out she needed.

"Yeah," she said, looking sideways at them. "I – I felt bad. I felt bad and I wanted to think things out, so I went for a walk. I went a long way, and it took longer to get back than I thought it would."

"Well, it's about time you realized the trouble you cause yourself – and everyone else too,"

Mrs. Watson said sharply. "I kept your dinner warm for you, though it would serve you right to eat it cold."

"Thanks," Marylee mumbled.

As though sorry she had scolded her foster child, Mrs. Watson hovered over her for the rest of the evening, until Marylee thought she would scream. She knew Mrs. Watson was feeling sorry for her again – flooding her with sympathy because she limped, because she had no home, because she was not bright and pretty and charming.

But it doesn't matter now, Marylee thought with contemptuous glee. She had April. Tomorrow morning, as soon as she could get out, she would go back to the warehouse where Petey was watching over her baby.

In bed that night Marylee didn't bother to look at the picture of the rushing stream. Her thoughts caressed the abandoned warehouse, the baby nestled in the makeshift cradle lined with her sweater and Petey's jacket. Tomorrow she would take the little bit of money she had saved and buy proper blankets and sleepers and things for April.

Everything had to be perfect for April.

Petey leaned against the wall of the warehouse with his arms clasped around his knees. He could feel the slow ebb of his courage matching the slow growth of the dark. It was always like this at night, waiting alone in the dark. No one was ever near, except Camper.

But at home he could at least set the television blaring, play a computer game, or go out into the streets with the other kids whose parents didn't care if they went to bed. Sometimes he even read a book – anything to keep the lonely darkness away for a while longer.

The baby stirred in the crate next to him, making the zipper of the jacket knock against the rough wood. Camper lifted his head, then slowly trotted over and looked into the box. Apparently satisfied, he returned to his place at Petey's feet.

"You're a better father than me, Camper," Petey murmured, rubbing the back of his dog's neck. "I don't know if I could stand it if you weren't here."

The baby stirred again. This time Petey looked into the cradle. His jacket had slipped off the child's shoulders as she moved about. Carefully he covered her up again.

"Hope it doesn't get too cold tonight," he remarked to Camper. His shirt wasn't very warm, but Marylee had impressed upon him that the baby had to be kept covered no matter what.

"Wish we could go home and watch TV," he muttered. He walked aimlessly to the window. It wasn't even late and already he was totally bored. Tomorrow he would bring his sleeping bag and a couple of comic books or something. He wished he had a phone to play games on.

The hours crept by. Occasionally Petey dozed, leaning against the wall. It became colder.

A dozen times he got up to leave. "Why should I stick around?" he demanded of Camper. But each time he started to leave, he stopped again. His father had left. He wouldn't be like his father.

Petey didn't know much about his dad. If she talked about him at all, his mother just said he was a no-good bum.

"He walked out because he thought all the fun had gone out of our relationship. He wasn't ready to give up the good times," his mother had told Petey once in a savagely bitter tone. "Fun! Where's the fun in raising a kid by yourself? What made him think I was having such a great time that he should just take off and leave us all alone? He hardly even sent us any money. And what could I do, saddled with an eight-month-old baby!"

The memory still made a cold, empty feeling of fear in the pit of Petey's stomach.

He was only eight when his mother had said that to him. For three days he cried, knowing that his father had taken off because of him and that his mother hated looking after him. On the third day he stopped crying and ran away. The police brought him back two days later.

Petey never forgot what happened when they brought him home. His mother came running out of the house, screaming his name. She hugged him and cried and cried; then she started slapping him so hard the police had to stop her. Finally she took him inside and made him bacon and pancakes even though it wasn't Sunday.

He remembered looking at her and seeing with surprise that she was white, that her makeup was gone, and that her carefully set hair was limp and dirty. Ugly bags had puffed up under her eyes.

"What's wrong, Mommy," he'd said. "Are you sick?"

Then she cried some more and he cried too. He told her how sorry he was she had to look after him when she hated it so much.

"Don't *ever* say I don't love you, Petey," she said fiercely. "Because I do! I could take off. I could walk out and have a good time, but I don't. I don't leave because I love you more than anyone else in the world. And if you ever run away again, I – I don't know what I'd do but you would never forget it. Do you hear me?"

He heard, and he understood that she wouldn't leave him.

But now Mike had shown up. Now she wanted to spend all her time with Mike. She said Petey was getting to be like his father – and she hated his father.

Just then the baby stirred again and began to cry. Petey walked over and stared down into the cradle. His dad had left when he was as little as April. Well, he'd show them. He wasn't like his dad....

The baby's wailing grew louder and louder. Her feet kicked and her arms waved furiously. With a convulsive heave, she flipped herself over and glared at Petey, screaming all the while.

"Okay! Okay!" Petey muttered. "Do you want a drink? How about some nice milk?"

The baby screamed louder.

"All right!" Petey snapped. "I'm getting it! I'm not used to this, you know!"

Camper paced anxiously, looking from Petey to the cradle. The noise of the cries grated on Petey's ears like fingernails on a chalkboard, making his hands clumsy as he tried to fill the bottle from the carton of milk.

"Damn!" he exploded as some of the milk spilled onto the dusty floor. Minute debris was carried along the tiny white rivulets.

"Here, kid, try this," he muttered when he finally got the bottle together. He shoved the nipple into the baby's mouth. She looked at him reproachfully, then began sucking. Her hands slapped at the bottle as she tried to hold it. Petey felt her small, warm forgers brushing over his as he held the bottle for her.

"Boy, you sure are greedy," he remarked.

The baby stopped sucking for a moment to smile at him. Petey laughed out loud, in spite of himself. The little girl seemed to be sharing some cheerful joke with him – something that went beyond words.

"I wonder who you really belong to," Petey said after a minute, his voice troubled. "Did your folks really ditch you like Marylee says? She's a little crazy – but maybe your parents both decided it was no fun looking after you and took off like my dad...."

Petey fell silent. April's sucking became slower and slower, finally stopping altogether. As her eyes drooped shut, Petey gently pulled the bottle from her lips. She sighed slightly and her cheeks and lips made sucking movements around nothing. Her breathing was slow and regular.

"Wish I could fall asleep like that," Petey muttered to Camper. He felt as though he had been in the warehouse for days rather than hours. Wearily, he settled himself back against the wall. He was just drifting off to sleep when the baby began to cry again. Even to his inexperienced ears this cry sounded different. But he was so tired. He just wanted to sleep.

The screams grew louder, more persistent. Reluctantly Petey stumbled to the cradle.

April's eyes were squeezed shut and her face was contorted. Perspiration stood out on her forehead and dampened her hair. Her body seemed to be stiffening. She pulled up her knees, all the while writhing and shrieking.

Petey froze. What was wrong with her? Why was she screaming like that? Maybe she was really sick...maybe something in her insides had broken from being carted around in a duffle bag.

"What's wrong, Camper?" he muttered desperately as he tried to pick the baby up. She writhed so much he nearly dropped her. The cries grew louder, more piercing – she seemed to have another attack. Convulsively her small hands grabbed at his shirt and she shrieked again and again in his ears.

"Hush, baby! Hush, baby! Hush...." Petey mumbled over and over as he walked back and forth across the floor. He couldn't stand the piercing screams, but he was numb from terror and helplessness. What was wrong? What could he do?

Suddenly the baby stiffened slightly, held up her head and emitted a long rolling belch, followed by two or three smaller burps. Then she sighed and snuggled her head against Petey's shoulder. In less than a minute she was sound asleep.

"I don't believe this, Camper," Petey whispered. "She just had gas. I guess I should have burped her or something after the milk. Boy, it sure isn't any fun looking after a kid...."

His voice trailed off. He hadn't meant to echo what his mother had said to him. It had just slipped out.

Well, it *wasn't* fun, he thought savagely. He hadn't asked for this baby – he was too young to have a baby to look after anyhow. Maybe he should take her to a cop, and too bad about Marylee.

The baby sighed slightly in her sleep and snuggled her cheek closer to the hollow of his shoulder. Her hands still clutched his shirt, but they were slowly relaxing.

"Do you think she'll wake up if I lay her down, Camper?" Petey whispered. Camper looked at him anxiously.

"I'll hold her a bit longer, just in case."

The warehouse was very quiet now. Petey's ears were filled with the soft sighs of the baby's breath. As he held her, Petey became reluctantly aware of new feelings growing in him. She was so helpless and she needed him so much.

"So who cares," he muttered roughly. The baby stirred. Automatically he made little soothing noises.

How could his father have left him when he was small and whispery like this little one? And why did his mother stay if it was always as horrible as it had been when the baby was screaming?

Everything was all turned around now in his mind.

Susan Brown

Chapter Four

Learning Happy

Marylee woke before dawn, still overflowing with the sensations of the day before. April was waiting for her. She must go to her baby.

But not yet, she realized fretfully. If she rushed off too early, there would be questions. They might find out. They might take April from her. Quietly she got up and dressed – she couldn't stand just lying in bed, staring at the grinning boy in the picture. Then for two long hours she sat on the edge of the bed, feeling her stomach turn sick with anxiety.

What if something had already gone wrong? What if Petey had got bored and just left April? She would become frightened, maybe even sick. She might become hysterical and choke.

"Oh, God," Marylee whispered, "don't let anything hurt April...."

At last she heard Mrs. Watson getting up and moving downstairs to the kitchen.

"Marylee!" she called as she passed the tightly closed door. "Time to get up! I won't have you lying around in bed all day just because you won't be going to school!"

"I'll just be a couple of minutes," Marylee responded in what she hoped was her normal voice. Wait a few more minutes to avoid suspicion. Keep yourself occupied.

She counted her money again. Eighteen dollars and seventy-five cents. It seemed like a lot, but she had never bought baby things before. Surely it would be enough. And maybe Petey had some more money too. They could manage fine.

"Marylee," Mrs. Watson called sharply up the stairs, "are you going to get out of that bed or not?"

"Coming! I'm coming!" Marylee called joyously. At last she could go.

At breakfast she maintained her usual silence, and as usual the Watsons checked the news and talked at each other. Rarely did either pay any attention to what was being said. They merely let words fly at random.

"Yankees won another game last night," Mr. Watson remarked. "Beat the Jays."

"News gets more upsetting every day," Mrs. Watson answered.

"I bet Jack Harris five bucks they'd win. The sucker always guesses wrong."

"It's really terrible."

"They've got the best pitchers. No doubt about it."

"Just look at this – a murder, a rash of burglaries and a kidnapping."

"That's what happens when you've got good pitchers."

"I'm going out," Marylee interjected quietly.

"That's fine, dear," Mrs. Watson said absentmindedly.

As Marylee went out the back door, she thought contemptuously that if she'd said she was going to rob a bank they wouldn't have noticed. But hurrying down the bleak street that led to the warehouse, she forgot all about them. April was waiting. Quickly she looked around to make sure no one was watching; then she slipped inside the squat building.

It was empty!

"No!" she cried wildly. Her knees felt weak. April! Where was April?

Then she heard a soft gurgling sound echoing from inside the remains of the warehouse office. April was still here! Petey must have moved during the night. For a moment she remained slumped against the dusty wall, weak-kneed with relief.

When at last she crossed to the office, she didn't even notice the harsh *shuuing* sound her foot made as it moved along the gritty floor.

Petey was asleep, his head pillowed on one arm. His other arm was draped across Camper. The old dog lifted his head when she came in, and thumped his tail on the floor. The baby lay in the crate, contentedly kicking her feet and examining the zipper on Petey's jacket.

"Good morning," Marylee whispered to her. April looked up and smiled cheerfully.

"Aah! Dee da daaah!" she gurgled.

Marylee knelt beside the crate and pressed her cheek against April's hand. She realized she had never been happy before – not even at that camp. But here in the dusty warehouse, shut away from the world, she felt an unfamiliar warmth, a sense of joy, stealing across her.

April looked up at her and cooed conversationally. Marylee let a breathless laugh slip from her. Then she reached her hands out for the tiny girl and lifted her up. April laughed and pulled happily at the thin strands of hair that hung over Marylee's shoulders.

"Are you hungry, baby darling?" Marylee murmured. "Would you like a little breakfast?"

Awkwardly balancing the baby on one shoulder, Marylee began mixing baby cereal with milk and fruit in a small jar left over from the child's first meal. She could have called Petey for help, but she didn't want him intruding on the perfect feelings streaming through her.

April watched Marylee mixing her breakfast with the same absorption she gave everything. When she realized it was her food that was being made ready, she began to whimper and jump in Marylee's arms.

"All right, April," Marylee laughed. "It's coming. You just sit in my lap and I'll feed you."

Marylee leaned against the splintery wall and April leaned against her. The meal was messy, but gloriously satisfying. April smeared the baby cereal across her face, and then pulled sticky fingers through Marylee's hair. To Marylee, the mess didn't matter – only the joy mattered.

The sound of giggling woke Petey up. Slowly he opened his eyes and blearily watched the meal in progress.

Stupid, he thought, to let the baby make such a mess. He wished they would shut up and let him sleep again. But the floor was too hard and too cold, and his body ached from twisting about, searching for sleep.

He had no energy to talk, and no desire to. So he just watched. He had never seen

Marylee smile before, let alone laugh, but he wasted little time on the thought. Everyone laughed at some time or other. After all, he'd only known her for one day. And besides, who cared.

"Ooh, you're wet," Marylee crooned softly to the baby. She sniffed the air. "I think you're dirty too," she mumbled with less enthusiasm.

Petey smiled slightly. He'd noticed the smell about an hour earlier, but there was no way he was going to change a dirty diaper. April didn't seem to care anyway.

"I guess I'd better change you," Marylee said reluctantly.

The baby smiled widely as Marylee spread out a blanket and laid her on it. Awkwardly, with growing distaste, Marylee pulled at the tapes that fastened the paper diaper together.

"Oh God!" she gasped as the diaper fell open. April giggled with elation and kicked her feet, catching one heel in the mess. Marylee tried not to breathe as she groped for the tissues to wipe the baby's bottom.

April giggled again and tried to roll over onto her stomach. Marylee caught her feet, but she continued to twist and squirm gleefully. Trying not to gag, Marylee pulled tissue after tissue from the container to wipe off April's bottom and heels. It was almost impossible to keep the mess off both her fingers and the blanket as the baby wriggled.

At last April was clean. Thankfully Marylee reached for another diaper, opened it, thrust it under the baby and wrapped it tightly around her. She dropped the dirty diaper and tissues into last night's grocery bag. Then, with careful thoroughness, she wiped her own fingers – again and again. Finally she threw the last tissue into the bag, and with a faint sense of triumph, folded over the top.

As she crouched down beside her baby again, Marylee noticed that Petey was awake.

"Hi!" she said, far too cheerfully. "Did you have any trouble with her last night?"

"A little. She cried some, but I burped her and it went away. I did okay," Petey muttered. He sat up and looked around. The bottle was still where he had left it. Hazily he remembered the warmth he had felt when the baby had snuggled her cheek into his shoulder, and he smiled slightly.

But then he moved. "Oh, crap," he groaned.

"What's wrong?" Marylee asked.

"I had to sleep on this stinking floor, that's what's wrong!" Petey snapped. "Everything in me aches."

"You'll get used to it," Marylee said indifferently.

"Like hell I will!" Petey shouted. "If you think I'm spending all my nights sleeping on a warehouse floor just to look after a baby you're even stupider than you look!"

"You have to," Marylee said, her voice a cold monotone. "You know I can't stay here at night. You know the baby can't be left alone. You know that. You've got to do it!"

"Why should I?" Petey yelled. "You're just like my old lady! You figure everything you want I'm just wild about. Well, I'm not. Why should I sleep on the floor and look after a kid who doesn't even belong here? You're crazy, you know that? That busted leg has affected your head. It's busted too if you think you can raise a baby in a warehouse!"

Desperate fear surged through Marylee. Things couldn't go wrong now. They just couldn't.

"Shut up!" she screamed. "You've got to stay! We've got to look after April!"

The baby's lower lip began to tremble, and her eyes squinted shut as the shouting grew louder. Suddenly she began to cry, sobbing furiously.

"Now look what you've done," Marylee snapped. "Your shouting scared her."

"My shouting!" Petey said derisively. "I didn't scare her. Here, give her to me."

He pulled April from Marylee's unwilling arms and nestled her against his shoulder.

"Okay, baby, take it easy. There's nothing wrong. Nothing's wrong."

He walked back and forth across the little office, his eyes staring triumphantly at Marylee as the baby settled down.

"You okay now, kid?" he asked softly. April made a few more noises at him, her tiny face twisted into an angry scowl.

"That's right," he laughed. "You tell us off good, kid."

Marylee watched them with narrowed eyes – hating him for quieting the baby, her baby. But she needed him. And years of being shuffled from one indifferent person to another had taught her a lot about getting what she wanted.

"You're pretty good with her," she said to Petey, the words nearly choking her. "I didn't know you were so good with babies. That's great. She's going to have two good parents now."

"Yeah, I am good with her," Petey said aggressively, "but don't you think you can con me." He glared at Marylee. "You should see the look on your face – like you'd kill me if you could. I'm not dumb either, Marylee, so don't try any con job. I'll stay if I feel like it, and that's it. So sit on it!"

Marylee glared back at him helplessly, hating him but feeling a grudging respect. He was just as tough as she was – in a different way maybe, but still tough.

"So what are you going to do then?" she demanded fiercely. "I'm going to keep this baby. No one wanted her – they just left her. And she wasn't lost, either. Nobody who cares about a baby carries it in a duffle bag, and you know it. So are you going to take off or not?"

Petey looked down at April. Her indignation forgotten, she was busily chewing his shoulder and muttering cheerful, nonsensical syllables. Yes, she did need him. And that witch Marylee needed him too – and she knew it.

"Maybe I'll stay. But you'd better watch it," he told her. The warehouse echoed his words. "I won't run out. I'm not like my fa – like some people. But you'd just better watch it. I'm in on this fifty-fifty, so don't try bossing me around. In fact, if I'm the father of this family, then I'm the boss."

"Oh, sure," Marylee said contemptuously, "some boss. You sure have a big mouth, Petey. Nobody's my boss and I'll bet your dad was never the boss at your house either."

Suddenly Petey felt tired. He wanted to cry. What was he doing here anyway, trying to play games?

But the baby needed him and he couldn't run out. It occurred to him that maybe, somehow, he could show his mother that she didn't need Mike – that her son was enough. This would prove it, wouldn't it?

He didn't want to look after a baby and he didn't want to hang around with Marylee. But if he took off the way he wanted to so badly, he would be just like his father. His mom hated his dad so much....

Now he knew what being trapped was like. There was no way out – he'd have to be April's father. Somehow, he thought. Somehow.

As usual the kitchen was full of the aromatic smell of morning coffee, but today Mrs. Watson was not aware of it.

"We mustn't have made Marylee very happy," she said in a troubled voice. Mr. Watson laid his tablet on the table and glanced at his wife in surprise.

"Why do you say that?"

"The closer it gets to the time for her to leave us, the happier she seems. This morning she actually laughed at a joke on the radio. A silly joke, but who knows what amuses kids these days? And when I heard her it occurred to me that in the six months she's been here I've never heard her laugh before – not once. In fact, I've never even really seen her smile."

"Don't be silly," he replied. "She smiles. We've both seen her smile."

"That's not a smile," Mrs. Watson said emphatically as she poured more coffee. "It's a caricature of a smile. It's as though she hates us so much she smiles to show it."

"That doesn't make any sense."

"I know, but it's true just the same. Like she was secretly stabbing us in her mind or something."

"You make it sound as though the girl's not right in her head."

"No," Mrs. Watson replied thoughtfully, "she's not crazy – at least not yet, though she might be some day with those kinds of feelings building up in her. It's more like she's been hurt so badly she's turned mean – like a puppy that's been kicked too much."

"You're imagining things," her husband said flatly. He picked up his tablet again.

"Maybe," his wife murmured. She rested her plump chin on her hand and looked out the window. "But I don't think so. Anyway, something's made her happy these last few days." She sighed. "I wonder where she's going every day. There's no point asking her. I just hope it lasts a while for her. Whatever it is, it's certainly what she's been needing all along."

"Hmmm?" Mr. Watson replied. "Hey, did you see this? The Yankees won again. That's another five bucks Jack owes me...."

The warehouse looked a little better now after a few days' habitation. Marylee had been able to wash the floor of the office after she discovered an outside faucet on another warehouse. The baby's crate-turned-cradle had been lined with foam and a flowered pillowcase stolen from Mrs. Watson's cupboard. An upturned crate had been lined with patterned wallpaper and covered with pink gingham. Inside it were several neatly folded infant sleeper sets. More pink gingham had been used to cover the outside of the cradle, and even the stained and cracked inner walls of the office.

Marylee had wanted to make curtains as well, but reluctantly abandoned the plan for fear that someone might investigate to see why pink gingham was fluttering from the broken windows of a warehouse.

Although she had never done much sewing before, and never any by hand, Marylee was determined to make everything pretty for

April. Yet, despite her good intentions, it seemed incredibly tedious sometimes – doing nothing but caring for the baby and trying to sew ruffles with unskilled fingers. But it never occurred to Marylee to stop. For the first time in her life she was filled with a sense of warmth, contentment and commitment that she guessed was love. She had expected dizzying rushes of emotion, but instead she felt a steady, warm outpouring.

Over and over again she repeated to herself that no one was as important as April. Dimly, as the minutes and hours and days slipped past, Marylee began to sense this reality – not in the words that danced through her mind, but as an intensity of purpose that superseded everything else. She forgot herself. The hate and bitterness began to crumble as warmth and caring spread through her being.

It was not yet summer, but for a few days the sun shone down brilliantly. With her baby in her arms, Marylee learned to laugh and to play silly little games. Lured out from the dark warehouse by the unaccustomed weather, she took April to bask in the sunlit warmth by the stream.

Gleefully April wriggled on the fuzzy blanket, waving hands and feet in the air as if trying to grasp an unseen butterfly. Marylee watched silently, delighting in the rippling movement of the baby's muscles under the soft, downy skin, and in the miracle of the perfect little body.

One day, after half an hour of enthusiastic waving and rolling over, April lay on her stomach, elbows and knees half stretched out, her tongue held firmly between her lips. Marylee watched breathlessly.

"Ah – daaah!" April remarked. Then with a sudden thrusting of her legs she pushed her bottom high up in the air and her nose firmly into the blanket.

"Careful! Don't hurt yourself," Marylee murmured anxiously, wanting to help but sensing she shouldn't.

April responded with grunting noises muffled by the blanket. Then slowly, shakily, like a newborn colt, she stiffened her elbows, thrusting her head and torso upwards until she knelt on all fours. Grinning widely, her blue eyes sparkling, she crowed to Marylee, all the while shakily maintaining this strange new position on her hands and knees.

"Oh, clever April!" Marylee congratulated her, sharing her glee. "You are the most intelligent baby, April! I don't think there's another baby in the whole world as clever as you are!"

Marylee dropped on all fours too, and carefully, with a wide grin, touched her thin nose to April's button nose. April laughed – a delighted, throaty gurgle. Then, shaking slightly with excitement, she waited for Marylee to play this new game again.

They touched noses again and again, each time laughing hilariously. Finally April's shaky arms and legs collapsed. Marylee scooped her up and cuddled her, kissing the top of her head and telling her over and over again what a wonderful little person she was, what a marvelously clever and greatly loved baby she was.

And now, somehow, even though Marylee still hated her limp, it didn't matter so much any more. April smiled at her and gurgled whenever she picked her up, never once looking at the thin, dragging leg. The limp simply did not exist for the baby, and so it no longer dominated Marylee's world.

As Marylee sat with her baby on the dreary bank, surrounded by squat factories and abandoned warehouses, she saw not a dying stream, but sparkles of living sunlight on the water and a haven where they lived in a family of loving and belonging.

"Well, April," she would whisper into the soft, sweet-smelling down of the baby's head, "what shall we do today? What wonderful things shall we do today?"

And April would laugh at the tickling whisper beside her ear, then reach around with her hands and touch Marylee's face.

Chapter Five

Promises

Mike's garage was white-painted and square – square windows decorated with faded signs and stacked up oil products, a square door that seemed clamped shut, and two square black caverns where cars disappeared to have their entrails taken out and welded back together again.

But there was a cheerful hum of activity too. From the depths came the blare of a radio, the roar of power tools, a medley of shouts and off-tune whistles from grease-covered mechanics. There was always a lineup of cars waiting to be ushered into the garage for repairs. Near the door, an inconspicuous sign stated that the garage was authorized by different agencies for inspections and repair work.

Petey leaned against the wall of the convenience store next door and chewed on some candy, trying to look casual, fighting an urge to run away. Why should he go in and humiliate himself?

"Damn him!" Petey whispered to himself, trying to work up a frenzy of hate that would give him an out. But there wasn't an out. Mike was his only chance.

They'd had the baby for just four days and already every cent he and Marylee had was gone. April drank milk constantly. It seemed that every time he turned around they needed something else for her – new diapers, clothes, sweaters, baby food, cereal. Marylee had borrowed a book about baby care from the library and they were relying on it to tell them what to do – and what they needed to buy for her.

Petey looked guiltily at the candy bar he was eating. The last of their money had gone for it – money that could have been used to buy one more jar of baby food.

He had to make some money fast. But where could a twelve-year-old find a job?

He didn't have any choice.

"C'mon, Camper," Petey said, nervously shrugging his thin shoulders.

He walked stiffly across the grey asphalt and pushed against the office door. It swung open easily, making a bell suspended above it jangle. An unshaven man dressed in overalls was chewing on a sandwich at the desk.

Petey cleared his throat. The man took another bite of the sandwich and stared at him.

"Is Mike around?" Petey asked, his voice sounding strange to his ears.

"Yeah." The man took another mouthful of his lunch. "In the back, through there." He jerked his head in the direction of a darkened door.

Petey hesitated a moment, then walked determinedly towards the door, Camper padding along behind him. Might as well get on with it.

His mother's boyfriend was standing with his back to Petey, talking to a mechanic who was wiping his hands on a greasy rag. "Give the owner a call before you start on any of those repairs, Eddy. He may want another estimate now," Mike said.

"Hey, Mike," Petey said loudly.

Mike turned around, his strong body pivoting easily among the tools and canisters on the floor. The light from the naked bulbs in the garage glinted over his blond hair and broad face. Surprise registered in his eyes when he saw Petey. Then he smiled.

"So, how are you doing there, Petey? And you too, Camper?" He leaned over to rub the dog's head. It irritated Petey that Camper obviously loved it.

"We're okay," Petey said shortly. "Can I talk to you about something? Privately," he added, glaring at the inoffensive mechanic.

"Sure thing," Mike said agreeably, looking at Petey keenly. "I'll make that call for you, Eddy. May as well take your lunch now."

Without any further conversation, Mike led Petey back to the small office in the front. The man with the sandwich was outside checking someone's tires.

"So, what can I do for you, Petey?" Mike asked calmly.

"I need a job," Petey blurted out. "I thought maybe I could do something around the garage."

Mike raised his eyebrows slightly. "You've told me often enough that you hate me," Mike remarked. "Why do you want to work for me?"

"I need some money – bad." Petey lifted his chin to stare at Mike. "I don't hate you especially, anyhow. I just don't like Mom spending all her nights off with you and leaving me alone at home. But I get by okay. You got a job or not?"

"Maybe. But first, let me get this straight. Your mom told me you stayed with friends at night." He looked at Petey quizzically, then added, "Do you spend the nights by yourself?"

So, Petey thought bitterly, his mother lied to Mike too. But he couldn't allow this guy to know she lied. Who did he think he was anyhow, putting his mom in a position where she had to lie?

"Yeah, well," Petey said unsurely, "last time the kid got the measles so they sent me home. They thought. Mom was there, but she was with you instead."

Mike looked at him sharply, then took a business card out of the desk and wrote something on it. He handed it to Petey.

"My cell number is on the back," he said. "If that happens again, call and she'll come home right away. You're too young to spend the night by yourself."

"Yeah, thanks," Petey said self-consciously, shoving the card into his pocket.

"So you need a job," Mike said briskly, sitting down on the edge of the desk. "I could use someone to answer the phone at lunch time. How about from twelve-thirty to one-thirty on weekdays – five dollars an hour – twenty-five bucks a week. Sound okay?"

"Yeah, great! Can I start now? I really need the money soon."

"You can start now if you want. I'll show you how to work the phone system. Say, Petey, you're not in trouble, are you?"

"Me?" Petey said, assuming an air of incredulity. "The only trouble I get into is at school. I – I'm just saving money for a bike. They cost a lot – the kind I want, I mean."

Mike looked at him but asked no more questions.

It didn't take long for Petey to learn what he had to know about taking calls. Mike told him he was good with customers, and Camper, stretched out on the sun-warmed office floor, watched his master approvingly. At the end of the hour, Mike gave Petey a twenty dollar advance.

Petey felt good, really good, as he approached the warehouse later in the day. He was doing it. He was making enough money to look after his "family." He knew now he wouldn't run out on them when they needed him.

The days passed by with an intensity of emotion and purpose that caused their previous lives to fade into a shadow of meaningless activity. Centered in their thoughts and activities was the baby – a miniature, adored ruler who waved chubby fists and gurgled and giggled and wept in heartbroken frenzies.

The morning April made her first attempt at crawling, Petey rushed out and bought ginger ale, then shook it so it foamed over the sides of the bottle like champagne in the movies. They laughed and carried on and spilled the pop as wildly as if they were drunk.

During the dark hours Petey cared for April. There were moments of great sweetness when he whispered his secrets and his hurts to her and to Camper, while she lay sleepily in his arms, her face nestled into his sleeve.

And there were frenzied hours when she screamed with gas, when the breezes through the broken windows became so cold that Petey covered her with his jacket and tried to stop Camper and himself from shivering in the thin sleeping bag. And there were the evenings when the guys were hitting baseballs and throwing footballs in the school field and he couldn't stay to play. Worst of all were the dreary, boring hours when it was too early for him to sleep but not too early for the baby. Then he had nothing to do except worry about how he was going to find the money to buy more baby food and diapers.

The twenty-five dollars from the garage didn't go very far, and every day Marylee found something new that the baby had to have – vitamins, diaper rash ointment, blankets, sweaters, teething rings, socks. The list was endless and he couldn't make her stop.

"She's nuts," Petey told Camper. "I guess the kid has to have those things, but where am

I going to get the money? I don't know how to get any more...."

Sometimes he became so frightened and desperate his hands shook. In his brain there was always the tempting chant that he could leave, let Marylee worry about it.

"I wish I could take off," he muttered for the hundredth time into Camper's sympathetic ear. "If only I could get out! How did I ever get into this anyway? I didn't want a kid...."

The walls of the warehouse echoed him, laughed at him because he "didn't want a kid." The whole universe was jeering, gloating at the trap that had been laid.

He was his father, saddled with a child he hadn't wanted, all the easy fun gone, maybe forever.

He was his mother, struggling to make enough money for the baby, sitting alone at night with a child who couldn't understand the waves of desperation and panic that seeped in with the dark and the shadows.

And he was himself – twelve years old and so scared he sometimes thought he was going to throw up.

It would be so easy to walk out, the little voice chanted – so easy. But it would be his father leaving him again. And it would be himself, abandoned completely by a mother who was tired of the work and the fears and the loneliness.

"So if I can just keep going," he murmured to Camper, "everything will work out right. It's got to be okay, if I don't take off."

The dog looked at him trustingly, sympathetically. Petey hugged him. "If I didn't have you...." he muttered. "You're the best dog ever. You're more than just a dog, Camper." Camper reached up his grizzled muzzle and licked Petey's face. Then they both snuggled into the sleeping bag and let the dark hours pass in sleep.

During the day, April belonged to Marylee.

Together they would play on the cemented area between the warehouse and the stream. Or Marylee would take the baby to the shopping mall to buy things for her, or to a park to swing and then sit in the cool grass.

If anyone asked Marylee why she was not in school, she had a story ready – she was new to the area, and because school was close to being finished, her parents had decided to wait until the fall to enroll her. April was a neighbor's child. She was babysitting, that was all.

Sometimes now, with a timid sense of wonder, Marylee would daydream about a family of her own. She hadn't done so for a long, long time – not since she had realized that no one would ever want her. But since she had found April, love had become a distant, flickering promise.

April needed her. Some day, when her baby was old enough to feel the emotion, that need would turn to love. At times now Marylee was almost sure that, perhaps some day, someone besides April would want her.

Sometimes she became caught up in the wonder of love and would laugh out loud and swing her baby through the air until April too was shrieking and laughing.

It was an idyllic time, encased in tumbledown walls and concrete, a time that made the half-remembered two weeks once spent at summer camp seem pale by comparison.

They had had the baby for almost three weeks now. Marylee hurried up to the front steps of the Watson's, cheerfully humming to herself. Halfway up the steps she hesitated. Through the screen she could see Mrs. Wojansky, her social services case worker. Generally Marylee didn't mind the woman. She rather liked her coarse-featured face, surrounded by soft brown, smartly set hair. She always wore the latest styles too, and Marylee liked that. She hated dowdy people because, with her lame leg, she was convinced she could never look good herself.

"What's she doing here?" she muttered to herself. She didn't want anything to interrupt the way things were going. Today wasn't the day for Mrs. Wojansky's regular visit. Quickly Marylee reviewed the last few days and decided she hadn't done anything to warrant the Watsons' phoning her case worker about her.

She hesitated only a moment longer. Might as well find out what was going on.

When the screen door slammed shut, everyone in the living room turned to look at her.

"Good evening," Marylee announced sarcastically.

There were two strangers, a man and a woman, sitting on the opposite side of the room. Both were middle-aged and, Marylee thought, rather dreary looking in their neat brown and beige clothes. She liked people who wore colorful outfits.

"Well, Marylee," Mrs. Wojansky said, assuming a friendly smile, "you know you shouldn't stay out so late without telling people where you're going."

"Shouldn't I?" Marylee said flatly, feeling all her old brittleness flooding back. There was a bad feeling in the room, maybe because they'd had to wait for her. She didn't care.

"Marylee likes her privacy and we haven't wanted to interfere, because she's been having such a nice time," Mrs. Watson hastily apologized.

Marylee dropped into an empty armchair and stared at the adults with carefully cold indifference. Inwardly she was trying to calm herself. *Take it easy*, she ordered her heaving mind. They don't know about April. They can't know about April!

"Marylee, this is Mr. and Mrs. Johnson," Mrs. Wojansky said.

Marylee's eyes flickered over them, but her expression remained unchanged.

"Hello, Marylee. Nice to meet you. We've heard a lot about you!"

Marylee said nothing.

"I'm afraid this young lady can be a little difficult when she wants to." Mrs. Wojansky gave her a sharp look.

But not when I'm with April, Marylee thought to herself. She didn't realize that a small smile wisped across her face, making her plain features lighten.

"Well, I'm sure we'll learn to get along all right," Mrs. Johnson said with a warm smile.

"What do you mean?" Marylee demanded, her voice flat and low.

"The Johnsons are going to be your new foster parents," Mrs. Wojansky told her. "You'll be moving in with them next Wednesday."

"No!" Marylee said loudly.

They're going to take you away! shrieked through her mind. They're going to take you away from April! April will be left alone!

She was breathing hard, trying to keep herself from screaming, from shouting obscenities at these people.

Be calm! she ordered herself frantically. You're not going yet. There's a whole week left to think of something. Be calm. You've got to work it out for April.

"I'm afraid you have no choice, Marylee," Mrs. Wojansky said briskly. "We told you weeks ago that we were looking for a new foster home for you. I'm sure the Watsons have been very good to you, and you've enjoyed being here. But you'll get equally used to the Johnsons. Besides, they have other foster children – you'll have some company and not have to spend so much time by yourself."

"That's just lovely," Marylee said, a cold edge to her voice, "but I'm afraid I'm not going. I'm staying. I like it here and I'm not going!"

"I didn't realize you had become so attached to the Watsons," Mrs. Wojansky said dryly.

"Yes, I – I have," Marylee said desperately. "They're terrific people. I don't want to leave them. I was just feeling settled, you know. I won't leave."

"Oh, Marylee..." Mrs. Watson said, her voice laden with pity.

"I won't go!"

"Now, Marylee," Mrs. Wojansky said firmly, standing up, "I don't know what kind of game you're playing, but it won't do. The Johnsons are looking forward to having you stay with them and that's all there is to it. I'll pick you up next Wednesday at nine, and I don't expect to be kept waiting. If whatever you have been doing the last few weeks is that important to you, I'm sure we can find a similar activity near the Johnsons', and if not, you could be driven over here occasionally. Now that that's solved, we'll say goodbye."

Marylee sat frozen in her chair. She did not hear the quiet discussion of her "problem" at the door. Nor did she hear Mr. Watson when he spoke to her as he switched on the television set.

Her mind was paralyzed. These people were going to take April from her. They were going to kill her, and they were going to kill April the same way.

She must have April! She could not live without her baby to love. She could not live through another day or week or month – or eternity – of the falsely sweet voices and concerned discussions, and year after year of being unloved and disliked and shunted from one place to another.

And April! Could she let them do the same thing to April? No! No matter what happened, she would protect April. No matter what.

Her mind was so full of April, she hardly heard the newscaster.

"Despite intensive police and volunteer searching, no trace has been found of six-month-old JoAnne Massey. However, early this morning police arrested twenty-three-year-old Alex Grayson of 121 Third Street and charged him with kidnapping the infant."

A police spokesman said that Grayson has confessed to abducting the child in order to extort a ransom from his former employers, Jean and Roger Massey. But the suspect claims he lost his nerve, and the day after the kidnapping left the infant in a duffle bag near the Massey factory on Porter Street, believing that workers would find the child and return her to her parents.

Workers, however, insist that no one saw either Grayson or the infant. Police investigators are working on the theory that an accomplice, probably female, still has possession of the child.

Our reporter spoke to the Masseys this afternoon. They are still clinging to the hope that their child will be found alive."

Vaguely Marylee saw the desperate faces of the man and woman on the television. She did not hear their plea to have their daughter returned. It was three hours later, when she was lying in bed, that what she had heard finally registered in her mind. April had not been abandoned! There was someone who wanted her.

But April...her daughter.... No! She could not, would not, give up her baby!

Chapter Six

Five Finger Discount

The morning air was dull, pressed down by the grey sky. As she struggled awake, Marylee could feel the weight, the greyness.

They were going to take her away from April.

For a while she lay in bed staring at the picture of the green wildness and hating that grinning boy. Then she tossed back the sheets and pulled her body out of bed. If they thought they could take April from her they were idiots, that's all – idiots!

A hundred improbable schemes jostled wildly through her thoughts as she dressed, ate breakfast and limped toward the warehouse. If only she could confide in Petey – but he'd just want to give April away, she thought scornfully. Somehow she had to think of a plan, a perfect, secret plan – one that would ensure his help before he realized what was really going on.

The plans continued to stumble through her mind in feverish disorder. She barely noticed Petey until he roughly blocked her way to the cradle.

"Marylee," he said abruptly, "there's no more money."

"What do you mean, there's no more money?" she answered impatiently, pushing at her drooping hair. What was he talking about? Didn't she have enough problems? They wanted to take her away from April...

She tried to push past him.

"I mean exactly what I said!" Petey shouted. "We've spent all the money! I only have eighteen cents left, and I don't get paid again until Friday."

"Well, borrow ahead or something," Marylee ordered. She peered down at her baby's sleeping face. April was so beautiful. How could she leave her?

"I did that last week," Petey snapped. "You've just got to stop buying things for a while, that's all. Will you listen to me!" He grabbed her arm.

Angrily she pulled free, her attention finally focused on him. "Well, what am I supposed to do?" she shouted scornfully. "Say, 'Gee, April, I know you're hungry, but we can't afford any more food until Friday when your dad gets paid. After all, it's only four more days.'"

"But I don't have any more money! Do I have to beat you over the head or something to prove it? I just don't have any more money! And I don't get paid for four days!"

"You sure aren't much of a provider," Marylee sneered. "You can't even make enough to feed one little baby. If I were you, I could do it!"

"Okay then, big mouth!" Petey screamed. "If you're so smart, then you do it! If it's that easy, just go ahead and do it! All by yourself, go ahead!"

Then he walked out, Camper trotting at his heels.

Marylee panicked – she had to have his help. Bitterly, she told herself how stupid she was. "Why can't you keep your big mouth shut?" she muttered. She limped to the door after Petey, but he was gone.

"What if he doesn't come back?" she whispered. "I mean, he's got to come back! He will come back!"

Defiantly she tossed her head and limped back to the cradle. April was stirring, muttering fretfully. She had to look after her baby.

"I hate her! I hate her so much I could do anything to her, and just laugh about it!" Petey raged to Camper.

He was sitting on a chunk of broken concrete, staring at the sluggish green of the stream. The sun had gone behind a cloud, so there were no silver and gold trickles of sunlight sliding across the murky water. Even if there had been, Petey was too wrapped up in his tumbling emotions to notice.

Camper sat beside him, whimpering his lack of understanding, shifting uneasily from one paw to another. He laid his muzzle on Petey's knee. Unconsciously Petey rubbed the dog's head and pulled at his soft ears.

"Doesn't she know that this whole thing is stupid?" he muttered. "How can I just keep getting more and more money? She's got to stop spending it – she's got to! What are we doing with a baby anyway? April must belong somewhere. It's crazy trying to look after a baby in a warehouse. And what are we going to do when it gets cold, and when she starts to walk, or if she gets sick or something? It's so stupid, Camper. It's so crazy stupid!"

Camper whimpered again, and slowly Petey got up and began meandering down the bank of the stream.

If only he could convince Marylee that it would be best to give up the baby. But he'd tried so many times and she just wouldn't listen. Listen! Jeez! Instead she would turn on him venomously, lashing his hurts until he felt sick and numb.

"It's as if she's crazy or something, Camper," he repeated. "She won't listen to me. I can't make her see how crazy it is to look after a baby like this."

For a long time he walked, eventually turning away from the bank and wandering down streets that were new to him. His thoughts never stopped spinning. It didn't matter what he did, there wasn't any way out – not unless he told about the baby himself. The thought surfaced again and again, but always in its train came his own sick fear of being abandoned. Somehow he couldn't unravel one from the other.

As Petey walked on, he found himself in a residential suburb of bungalows and Tudor style homes. All the kids he saw on the street seemed to have new bicycles and sharp little voices. The neighborhood was totally different from the rows of brown, three-story houses crowding toward broken sidewalks where he lived.

He and his mom had the whole first floor of one of those houses. The odd shaped, too large and too small rooms, painted with dull beige and green paint, felt comfortable to him. He wondered if the children lived in beige rooms here, or if they had bright rooms with flowered curtains and cute stuffed animals spread around. With a half-smile, he wondered if their beds creaked the way his did. How long had it been since he'd slept in it?

His thoughts slid back to the baby. April needed food, and somehow he had to get it. He wondered for a moment if any of the people in these expensive homes worried about how they would get the money to buy food and diapers for their babies.

"Not much chance, is there, Camper?" he muttered.

He continued walking, still not knowing where he was going, feeling determined and hopeless at the same time. He knew that somehow he would manage. If only he knew how.

The street he was on broadened suddenly. There were sidewalks now, and the trees were just saplings, wired to poles and surrounded by little mesh fences. A couple of blocks farther on he could see a shopping center. He headed toward it, keeping an eye out for returnable pop bottles. Around his home there were usually a few that people had dropped by the side of the road. In this district, though, he saw only cans.

Even the grocery store in the plaza was unlike the one in his neighborhood. Instead of dim piles of goods and crowded aisles where old men shuffled and kids ran, this store was brilliantly lit, full of orange and red banners. Cynically, Petey thought it looked like a cross between a carnival and a gift shop. The shoppers were different too, less tired looking, moving quickly down the wide aisles. None of them even glanced at him.

Out of habit he walked to the baby food section. There were hundreds of jars piled on the shelves in neat unbroken rows.

So much food....

Suddenly Petey became angry. There was so much food here and April needed it so badly. He chose four jars and hastily shoved them into his wide jacket pockets. There were no shoppers in the aisle to see him, and even if there had been, he knew they wouldn't have looked at him long enough to notice.

Quickly he walked out of the store. At any moment he expected shouts behind him and heavy hands grabbing at his arms. Nothing happened. No one had noticed.

With Camper padding behind him, he began the long walk back to the warehouse. He had food for April, but he didn't feel good about it. He felt cold and scared.

"They've got loads of stuff," he told Camper gruffly. "They won't even miss it."

But he knew he didn't care whether they missed it or not. It was him. They weren't hurting, but he was. He felt awful.

Lots of kids swiped things from stores, Petey told himself, only they didn't call it stealing – it was "a five finger discount" or "ripping off" or any of several other names for it. Petey faced it coldly: he had stolen the food.

He had never stolen anything before, not even with the other kids. It had always seemed stupid and mean, because he knew the owners of the little stores near where he lived. Petey wondered if he would have felt so awful if it had been an idle joke, the way most of his friends picked things up – a sort of "to hell with you" defiance. But this hadn't been like that. He had felt so desperate, and he hadn't wanted to steal. Maybe that was the difference – this wasn't some kind of game. He knew now that if he were caught no one would think of it as a kid's game, or say something stupid like "boys will be boys." He decided not to think about what would happen when he got caught.

Petey had a strange certainty that it wasn't a matter of if. It was simply when. As he slipped in the door of the warehouse, he could hear the baby crying.

It had been only four days since he had

first stolen food, but as Petey sized up this store, he felt as though he had been doing it for a long time. He had cut off his emotions and now just went coldly by whatever Marylee said they needed.

But the emotions were still there, underneath. They came ripping through in the quiet of the night, setting his hands shaking and his heart pounding. But it was cold daylight now, and he didn't choose to think about it.

Marylee had told him that morning that they needed another baby blanket or a bunting bag. Petey had been unsure of what that was, but he had looked around the children's wear department of the store and now he knew. It was a snowsuit for babies, without legs in it – just like a sleeping bag with a hood and arms.

He was already loaded down with baby food, and not sure how he could get a bunting bag out too. But he would manage somehow. He was a good provider and he would manage.

He missed having Camper at his heels, but dogs weren't allowed in the store, so he had left him sitting patiently by the door. Camper would wait until his master came back out and called him.

But right now Petey had to get the bunting bag. There was a bright red one on the sale counter, just the right size. That was the one.

He went into another department in the store and bought a large shopping bag for a dollar. The bag was emblazoned with the store's insignia and he hoped it would look as though he had bought the baby things. Hastily he put the jars of baby food in the bag so it would lose its empty look. Then he walked back to the children's department.

The salesgirls were leaning against the counter that held the cash register, idly gossiping. Petey heard one of them launch into an excited account of what a fantastic guy she was dating.

Trying to look unconcerned, he wandered aimlessly around the display counters. He picked up and put down first one thing and then another. Finally he picked up the bunting bag. He looked around surreptitiously. No one was nearby except a woman carrying a shopping bag, looking at some children's T-shirts.

Holding the bunting bag so that his body shielded it from the eyes of the salesgirls, he walked quickly out of the department. He paid no attention to the other shopper. Once out of the department he walked away from the racks and quickly stuffed the garment into his shopping bag. He breathed a sigh of relief. No one had seen him.

As always, he felt sick to his stomach and a little cold as he walked toward the door leading to the street. One more time. He had managed one more time.

"Here, Camper!" he called. The dog trotted up to him. But just as Petey leaned down to pet him, hard hands grabbed his arms.

Frantically he looked up. A man in a business suit, and incredibly, the woman shopper from the children's wear department were looking at him grimly and holding tight to his arms.

"Hey! What's the big idea!" Petey said loudly, feeling his heart knocking against his ribs and seeing a small crowd gathering on the street. Desperately he tried to pull away, but they just held on to him more tightly.

"I think you had better come up to my office, young fellow," the man said coldly. "We want to ask you a few questions."

"What's happened?" someone in the crowd asked.

"Oh, they just caught a kid shoplifting, that's all," another voice answered.

"I didn't do anything," Petey cried frantically, yanking his body back and forth in an effort to get away from them.

"You might as well come along on your own feet, because you are coming whether you want to or not," the woman said.

"Let go of me!" Petey shouted desperately. The cold indifference was gone. He was so scared he thought he would be sick. Over his shoulder he saw Camper trotting anxiously behind him.

They took him up three escalators and into an office with two steel chairs and a steel desk against one wall. The man sat down behind another desk and faced Petey.

"Well, son, what's your name?" he said.

"None of your damn business," Petey snapped. It was like the principal's office, he thought dimly, only worse. A thousand times worse.

"There's no point in being difficult," the woman said quietly. "After all, I saw you take the baby clothes. Sit down in that chair" – she pointed to a grey metal chair – "while we make a couple of phone calls and fill out some forms."

The man pulled the forms out of his desk and handed them to the woman. She pulled the other chair up to the metal desk, sat down and began writing.

"I'm afraid we're going to have to call the police," the man said. "It's our store's policy to prosecute all shoplifters, no matter how young they are."

Petey sat unmoving on the chair. Everything was spinning around in his head. He was so scared....

They'd never understand. How could he ever explain about the hungry baby and how his father had left him and that his mother would rather be with Mike. He hated them all! Didn't this man know what it was like to be desperate? Had he ever tried to look after a family when he was only twelve years old?

Petey wanted to scream and swear at these people who didn't know and didn't care. And he was so afraid.

"The police are sending someone over from their juvenile department," the man said as he put down the phone. "When you finish your report, Mrs. Haigle, you may as well go to lunch. I'll look after things here."

After the woman left, Petey and the man sat in silence. Petey had caught a glimpse of Camper sitting morosely beside some boxes just outside the door. Apparently no one had noticed him.

It seemed to the boy like a sweating eternity of cold silence as they waited for the police. The man asked him one more time what his name was.

"Go to hell," Petey said, but his voice was little more than a whisper.

At last the police officer came. He looked with indifference at Petey. He didn't notice Camper slipping through the office door before he shut it, and sneaking under the desk.

"We've got another one for you," the man said with a grim look. "You'd think their parents would clamp down on them. Wouldn't catch my kids shoplifting."

The policeman shrugged.

"Okay, son. Stop causing trouble and maybe we can get this sorted out. First of all, what's your name and where do you live? Secondly, why baby clothes? Did you do this on a stupid dare or something?"

"A dare!" Petey shouted wildly. "You don't know anything, damn you! The warehouse is getting cold again and the baby was hungry. I had to get the things for the baby!"

"Now just a minute, son," the policeman said sternly. "You watch your language!"

Petey glared at him, felling the tears rolling from his eyes. He jammed his hands into his pockets.

"You stinking bastard!" he whispered.

"I told you to watch your language," the policeman retorted, yanking Petey's hands back out of his pockets. A piece of paper fluttered to the ground. Miserably, Petey recognized it as Mike's business card.

But before he had a chance to worry about it, he heard a low growl. Camper, who had been anxiously crouching under the desk, suddenly lunged forward, sinking his teeth into the policeman's arm.

"Hey! What – " the officer shouted, clutching his arm.

Petey ran for the door and flung it open, hesitating only long enough to scream, "Camper! Here, boy!"

Together they raced along a hallway and down the back stairs. Frantically they tore out of the store and onto the street.

For as long as they could, they ran. And finally, when they were both too winded to go any farther, they crouched in the wild shrubbery of a park for half an hour, until at last Petey felt it was safe to come out.

"Good boy," he murmured brokenly to Camper. "There's never been another dog in the whole world like you, fellow."

Then they began the long walk to the warehouse, both so tired they felt as though their feet were encased in lead.

Chapter Seven

Leaving Home

Four days had gone by. Four days and still the plan was frighteningly hazy.

Marylee knew they had to run away. But where? Where could they find a home? And how could she convince Petey to come with them? Ever since the day they'd had that argument about money he had been acting strange.

She knew he would come back that day, but she knew she had handled him all wrong too. So when he silently handed her the four jars of baby food, Marylee put on her best "Aren't you terrific!" act.

"Wow, that's great," she forced herself to say. "I knew you'd do it!"

Briefly Petey glared at her, hate searing out of his eyes.

"Stuff it!" he said tersely. "I did it, so don't hand me any of that 'Aren't you wonderful' crap. I told you before that you can't con me, so don't try. I'm doing what I have to do, that's all. So just stuff yourself!"

Marylee eyed him for a minute, wondering what she would do next. It occurred to her that she ought to apologize. The thought was a surprise – she never apologized to anyone unless it got her something she wanted. Before April, she had never cared how anyone felt about what she did.

"Well, you can just stuff yourself too," she replied tartly. "But you did do okay and I guess I shouldn't have yelled at you. So there's your 'wonderful you' crap." She felt her face reddening and bitterly wished she hadn't exposed herself with that half apology.

Petey looked at her. His eyes were mocking, but his mouth half smiled. "Awesome," he muttered. "I'm going home. I'll see you later."

He had been back on time, the same as always. But he had acted a little different – more sarcastic, harder.

So who cares? Marylee told herself. As long as he sticks it out – who cares?

So far, she had been sure she could count on him. But she remembered, with a flash of uncertainty, how he had reacted earlier that morning when she gave him her carefully thought-out list of things – things she knew they would need to run away with. He read the list aloud, but stopped at the bunting bag.

"Marylee," he said, his voice trembling slightly, "we don't have to have all this stuff, do we? I mean, couldn't you just hold off a little?"

"No, I couldn't," Marylee snapped. She didn't want to give away her plan, not yet. "It's – it's supposed to turn cold tonight. Of course, if you don't care if April freezes...."

Petey's face hardened with resentment, but he left without saying anything else.

Marylee had watched him go with relief. The way he acted about getting things made her uncomfortable somehow. Now that he had gone, she and April had a whole beautiful day ahead of them.

But since then everything had gone wrong.

April started crying while her diaper was being changed, and went on whining and crying all morning until Marylee wanted to scream at her in frustration. Guiltily she tried to stifle her feelings and make an extra effort to play with April, but the baby sobbed as though her heart were breaking. Marylee asked herself what she had done wrong. Why didn't April want her any more? Desperately she consulted her book.

The book suggested a variety of problems – ear infection, viruses, teeth. April screamed miserably.

"Please stop crying, April," Marylee pleaded. "You know I'm trying to help."

April only cried louder.

For the first time since she had found the baby, Marylee's buried doubts surfaced for a moment. What did she know about mothering – a girl who had never had a mother? But then April lifted her face to her and cried so plaintively, so plainly saying how miserable she felt, that Marylee slammed the doubts down again.

April needed her, and no one else could need the baby as much as she did. After all, Marylee told herself, that woman who had lost April could have another baby. Besides, if they really cared about their baby, how could they have allowed her to be kidnapped?

It was plain that Marylee should keep the baby.

April cried again and rubbed fretfully at her eyes. Trying to find some kind of remedy in the book, Marylee paced back and forth in the warehouse office with the complaining baby squirming on her shoulder. If teeth were the problem, it said, there would be bumps on the lower gums where they were about to burst through.

Marylee sat April on her lap and tried to look into her mouth. April screamed furiously and slapped at Marylee's hands.

"April, please. I'm trying to help. You know I wouldn't hurt you!"

The baby opened her mouth and wailed miserably. The sound grated unbearably on Marylee's ears, but she got a glimpse of the lower gum. There was a thin white line where a tooth had begun to break through, and a sore looking lump beside it. A second tooth was pushing against the gum as well.

"Poor little April," Marylee murmured, gathering the baby up in her arms. "Your poor little mouth is sore."

April cried again and hit out with her hands. She kneaded the skin of Marylee's cheek as her fingers grasped convulsively. Marylee hissed when the sharp little nails scratched her.

"Ow! Don't!" she snapped. Startled by the loud voice, April began sobbing even more furiously, clutching at Marylee's collar. Marylee sighed and wondered when Petey would come. It was going to be a very long day.

While she walked the floor, wearily shifting the baby from one shoulder to the other, Marylee feverishly filled in the details of her plan. They would run away with the baby – upstream into the wilder country she knew lay several miles outside of town. There they would be safe.

"We'll live near trees – they're good and loving, like us," she whispered to April. "There'll be wild berries and fruit, and a nice warm cave or something to live in. And even if it's hard to find things to eat," she added hastily, "I can do without food for a few days till we get close to a town where Petey can get some kind of job. We'll manage just fine."

Marylee told herself so many times that this was the only way, she almost started to believe it. It wouldn't be long now before the police found out, somehow, about April. Someone would hear her crying, or Petey's mother would find out he was gone every night, or else the police would simply reach the warehouse in the course of their massive search. She had to keep April from them. They had to run away.

"It's a great plan," she told herself again.

The sky was beginning to darken, filling with oppressive grey clouds, when Petey finally burst into the warehouse. Marylee was sitting on the floor feeding April a messy dinner of strained meat and vegetables when she heard Petey's heavy footsteps and the click, click of Camper's nails on the cement floor.

"Did you get everything?" she asked without looking up from the difficult task of it just came out. I talked about the baby and I think I said something about the warehouse."

"You idiot!" Marylee screamed, jumping to her feet. "You stupid idiot! They'll find us now! And we're not ready! They'll take April away! Don't you see, they'll take April! We've got to go," she said wildly, rushing around and grabbing everything within reach of her hands.

April watched the frenzied action and her lower lip began to tremble. Suddenly she let out a loud wail of fright.

The cry pierced through Marylee's panic. Strangely, it calmed her. She scooped up the baby.

"Hush, darling," she said softly, holding April close to her. She felt the familiar rush of loving and needing. And she felt a searing need to weep out a broken heart.

Don't be silly, she whispered to herself. Nothing has happened yet. And it won't anyway, because I won't let it.

"We've got to get out of here," she told Petey in a calm but strained voice. "I have it all planned. We'll follow the stream out of town and up into the woods. We'll be safe there. Once we're safe, we can plan what to do next."

"No!" Petey said desperately, unbelievingly. "Don't you see what's happened? Your game of playing house is over. The police will find us.

maneuvering the spoon between April's hands and into her mouth.

"No, I didn't," Petey said in a strange voice. Marylee looked up quickly. He was deathly white, and his eyes looked bleary, as though he had been crying.

"What's wrong?" she demanded. "We have to have those things!"

"Well, we'll just have to do without them!" Petey said savagely. "I can't get them. I don't have any more money and I – I can't get them the other way anymore." His voice shook as he raised frightened eyes to Marylee.

"I – I got arrested for shoplifting," he cried, his voice still quivering. "Camper bit them so I got away. But they'll find me easy. I know they will. Mike's phone number fell out of my pocket."

Marylee's heart started pounding faster and faster.

"You – you didn't say anything about April though, did you?" she asked, her voice barely above a whisper.

April gleefully reached out and knocke the jar of food over. Marylee hardly notic as the baby splatted her fingers in the goc mess.

"Yeah, I did," Petey said harshly. The stared sadly at April. "I – I didn't mean to

They'll find the baby and – and they'll find me too! I'm probably going to have to go to jail or juvie or something, Marylee," he cried, a rising note of hysteria in his voice. "I stole for you and for the baby. I did what I was supposed to do! I was a good father – I was everything a good father is! I looked after her all night when it was cold and dark, and I held her when she cried. And I even stole for her, to feed her! I did everything and now it's done with and I think I'm going to have to go to jail!"

Finally his voice broke and he ran from Marylee into the shadows of the far corner of the warehouse.

With an icy sense of shock she realized he was crying. Marylee didn't know what to do and the panic began rising in her again. She couldn't give up April. But what had she done to Petey? She'd not really thought much about him before. He hadn't mattered. He'd been there and she had used him – and now he might go to jail because of her.

"Oh, April," she whispered, laying her cheek against the baby's head. Tears streamed down her cheeks.

With all the misery of the past years, she had never before felt so sad and lonely. Those years had been full of hurts, hurts that she had turned into hate. But now she was full of love turning into loneliness, and it felt much more terrible than anything she had known before.

They would come for April soon. But she had to keep April. She had to keep the baby because no one else in the world would ever love her again.

"Petey!" she called imperiously, feeling a rush of purpose again.

"Go to hell!" he shouted back. She heard Camper whimpering in the shadows.

"Petey!" she called again, more strongly. "You've got to help. It's our only chance now. I'm taking April away and we need you to help. Don't run out on us now! Please! And – and then the cops won't find you either. You won't have to go to jail because no one where we're going will know that you were shoplifting. All they'll know is that you're doing what a father should...."

Her voice trailed off. She didn't know what else to say to Petey to convince him. There was a long moment of silence, then Petey came toward her from the shadows.

"You sure are full of crap," he told her viciously. His face was white and streaked from crying.

"No," Marylee said. "No, we really need you now. And you've really done good all along. I should've told you before but I never thought of it. Even if you don't come I've got to go because

I can't – I just can't let them take April from me. She's all I've got."

Petey looked at her for a moment longer, his eyes narrowing at the tears he saw in her eyes. Awkwardly he reached out his hand and stroked April's soft hair. Then he sighed and turned away.

"Okay," he said wearily, "let's get started."

The clouds that had scudded across the late afternoon sky had banked up in heavy grey masses as far as they could see. Marylee hitched her bundle into a more comfortable position and looked back for a moment into the warehouse. The pink gingham frills around the empty cradle fluttered briefly in the breeze that was puffing erratically through the window. The building looked strange now with no baby or baby clutter in it.

"Hurry up!" Petey called impatiently from the side of the stream.

"Coming." Marylee limped resolutely through the door. Why did she feel she was leaving home forever?

"I never had a home," she whispered to herself. She looked ahead at Petey, April and Camper waiting for her by the stream. Abruptly Marylee felt a surge of triumph and joy. Her family....

"Let's go," she said quietly. The others followed silently as she limped upstream.

The concrete banks along the stream were broken and hard to walk over. Nondescript plants, resembling grass, sprouted scrawny leaves from between the cracks, as nature tried to heal herself. For an hour they passed factories, small businesses and warehouses, all square and squat and alike in the gathering shadows.

Once Marylee looked at the sky. The clouds were thick, making sunset appear to come earlier than it should.

"It's going to rain," Petey panted behind her. He had been carrying April, but her weight was becoming more than he could handle.

"No," Marylee said flatly, "it won't. We'll rest for a while now."

Silently they sat down against the wall of one of the buildings. Marylee began to massage her weak leg. So much walking was putting a strain on it, making it ache. She refused to think of how it would feel in a few more hours. Somehow she would keep going until they were safe. She looked over at Petey.

April was asleep, had been for the whole trip, her head lying loosely on Petey's shoulder. Only her face was showing, and that barely, so carefully had she been wrapped in blankets and a layer of plastic to keep off the threatening rain.

"How you doing, old fellow?" Petey was murmuring to Camper, rubbing the dog's ears.

Camper's tail thumped slowly but he didn't move much.

"He sure looks beat," Marylee said.

"Yeah," Petey replied, the worry sounding in his voice. "He's pretty old and I think sleeping on the warehouse floor has sort of tired him out."

"Where did he sleep before?"

"In bed with me. He's always slept with me."

"He'll probably be okay," Marylee said, suddenly hoping it was true.

"Yeah," Petey replied unsurely. "I mean, he's one tough dog. But he seems so tired lately – kind of like all the snap has gone out of him."

"The woods will be good for him then. You know how people always go to the country for their health."

Petey looked at her contemptuously. "Yeah, nothing like a country resort to get a dog back on his feet. Cut it out, Marylee. I haven't backed out and neither has Camper."

Marylee flushed. For a moment she hated Petey and his invariably accurate awareness of the manipulation behind her words.

"Well, we ought to get going." She pulled herself awkwardly to her feet.

"Yeah," Petey answered, sighing as he stood up. Marylee felt a wave of guilt, but angrily pushed it away. After all, she hadn't made him come, or help look after April.

But the realization came just the same. She had manipulated Petey. The worst of it was, she thought slowly, that he knew she had used him – had pulled on whatever it was that made him feel he had to play the father. Marylee bit her lip, feeling slightly ashamed of herself and sorry for the bad trouble Petey was in. Every time he had harped on the words that put the dead look of fear in his eyes, the words that both rewarded and terrified him.

"Gaa – daadadaaaa – ga!" She heard April crooning to herself from her perch on Petey's shoulder. Quickly she looked around. April was sitting up in Petey's arms, alertly looking around, chewing one finger and talking to herself. When she noticed Marylee watching her, a smile spread across her face, widening into a grin of cheerful companionship.

Marylee's heart flooded with joy and she gasped slightly as a breath of pure happiness caught in her throat. Her remorse was forgotten, washed away in the flooding adoration of the baby – her baby.

Everything would be just fine.

Chapter Eight

On the Run

They had been walking steadily for almost three hours, trying to get as far as they could before exhaustion forced them to stop.

As before, there was no conversation, but now it was from weariness. The ache in Marylee's leg had become a torture, but she was determined not to stop. If once she sat down, she was afraid she wouldn't be able to go any farther.

"Time for a rest," Petey said finally. His arms ached from carrying April, but he was more worried about Camper. The old dog was walking along stolidly, but he was whimpering frequently, his head hanging down.

"Just a bit farther," Marylee forced herself to say.

"No," Petey insisted flatly. He headed toward a tree. "Now."

Too weary to argue, Marylee limped over and sat down beside him, her back to the huge tree. Camper flopped down, his head and front paws over Petey's outstretched legs, and appeared to fall asleep instantly.

Marylee silently took the now sleeping April from Petey's aching arms and looked out at the stream.

In the hours they had been walking, the scenery had changed dramatically. Under their feet the concrete had gradually become older and more broken, until it had finally disappeared in a tumble of weeds.

The factories had also been left behind, replaced by tumbledown wooden houses in cluttered yards. The children from the houses had eyed them silently, indifferently, as they stumbled by. Later there had been a green schoolyard and then a long stretch of well-cared-for bungalows, a small park, and finally larger, more impressive homes.

These too had petered out, until now the trees crowded close to the stream and the undergrowth was thick and ragged. Through the trees they could see gaudy billboards announcing that the land was divided into lots, available for purchase – the site of the new Devonshire Estates.

But except for regularly placed survey stakes with fluorescent plastic flags, there was no sign that anyone was about to live there.

Marylee thought the trees and shrubs seemed a bit desperate, as though they knew they were there by sufferance and would soon be destroyed. It seemed an unhappy place, not like the woods she had loved.

The stream had changed as well. It had lost its air of furtive decay and now flowed smoothly between overhanging banks. Occasionally it laughed and rushed over outcroppings of glistening rocks.

"It's going to rain." Petey broke into her thoughts. "We'd better find some shelter."

"It won't rain."

Petey said no more, but there was a sudden flurry of drops in the leaves of the trees. It had become so dark they could hardly see each other. "We've got to find some shelter," he repeated, exhaustion making his voice listless.

"Which way?" Marylee asked unsurely as they scrambled to their feet.

"There's nothing behind us," Petey answered, "and I can't see anything ahead in this blackness. Let's cut over to the road. Maybe there'll be a barn or shed or something."

They trudged toward the road as more and more raindrops splattered against them. Rivulets of water began to run over their faces and seep into their clothes. Marylee held April against her, trying to keep the rain off the baby's face. She hoped the plastic would keep her baby dry.

She looked behind and saw that Petey was carrying Camper, trying to protect him from the cold rain with his coat, while balancing their bundle of baby things in his other hand.

They walked on. The rain began to pound down, harder and harder. The road, when they reached it, was deserted, with no buildings in sight. They kept walking.

"I see something," Petey said finally. Marylee hardly heard him. Her mind was reeling with exhaustion and the pounding desperation of keeping April safe and warm.

It was a building – an old gas station, long since closed down when the main highway moved west of the road they were now on. The windows and door were securely boarded up, but grateful for any shelter, Marylee huddled with April in the narrow indentation of the doorway.

"Break in," she ordered Petey flatly.

He looked worriedly at Camper, then carefully laid him on the stoop, out of the rain. He pulled off his dripping jacket and laid it over the animal's heaving sides. Marylee crouched down beside the old dog and rubbed his head.

"I'll look after him," she said, hoping April would not wake up.

Petey nodded and disappeared.

She could hear him pulling at the securely nailed boards; then she saw him walking purposefully along the road. He reappeared a couple of minutes later with a bent piece of rusted metal about a yard long. Soon, from the other side of the building, she could hear scraping and banging through the dripping noises surrounding her.

There was a loud, snapping crunch; then Petey reappeared at Marylee's side.

"I broke the edge off the wood," he said briefly. "I think we can get in."

The break in the boards was jagged-edged and almost shoulder high. "We'll have to put April and Camper down," Petey told her. "I'll boost you up and hand them in to you. I'll be able to get in by myself."

"I can't put her down in the mud!"

"Then you can stand out here in the storm with her all night!"

They glared at each other through the dark and the rain. Then, reluctantly, Marylee laid April down beside the building, trying to put her in what little shelter the wall provided. Camper had not moved from the doorstep.

Petey made a cup of his hands, and unsurely Marylee tried to use them as a step. She had seen kids do this at school, but she had never tried it before. It felt terrifyingly unsteady.

"Hurry up!" Petey grunted.

"I'm trying!"

Her lame leg was unwieldy, but somehow she got it through the jagged break. Straddling the wall, she could feel the agony of broken splinters pressing against her legs through her jeans. Finally she drew her good leg through and balanced precariously, half sitting on the bottom edge of the hole.

"Jump!" Petey shouted angrily. Couldn't she do anything?

Marylee looked into the yawning blackness of the building. No light pierced the gloom.

"I – I can't!" she said hoarsely. "There's no light. I can't see what I'm jumping into. And besides I don't think my leg can take it."

"If you don't jump, I'm going to push you!" Petey said through clenched teeth.

"April and Camper have got to have shelter. Or have you forgotten your precious baby already?" Petey glared up at her. Marylee raised her arm as if to defend herself from his words.

Jump, she told herself. *You've got to jump!*

I can't! I can't! screamed through her mind. Then for a horrifying instant Marylee saw herself as one of the uncaring faces – one of the well-meaning people who really didn't care when it mattered. April...Did she really care about April?

Frantically she looked down at Petey and April. Then she peered into the blackness. She could feel her weak leg shatter as she fell on it. She could hear the snap and her own scream as she fell on and on into the blackness.

"I'll push you!" Petey shouted, putting a warning pressure on her back.

"No! no!" Marylee pleaded.

Then she looked back at the baby, and the love rose above her exhaustion and fears. April had to have shelter. She shut her eyes, swung her good leg out awkwardly, until it hung in the blackness, and pushed herself off.

She grunted painfully when her drawn up body hit the floor. It had been a short fall, only about a yard. With dull relief Marylee realized there had been no snapping bone, no permanently crippled body – only scrapes and bruises from her awkward fall.

Slowly she stood up and leaned her head and arms out the hole to take her baby. As Petey picked April up, a puddle of cold water cached in the plastic suddenly escaped and streamed over her face. She screamed, her cries louder and wilder with each second.

Wordlessly Petey handed her over. Marylee held the baby against her body, muttering soothing words, but she cried on and on, howling in outrage and rising hysteria. Reluctantly, Marylee laid her down to take Camper from Petey. Even when she was picked up again, April continued to scream. Uncertain what was wrong, Marylee felt the baby's clothes under the plastic – they were soaking wet and bitterly cold. Quickly she pulled them off, fumbling in the dark, trying to hold the wriggling, shrieking child. When the baby was naked, Marylee searched through her bundle for dry clothes and diapers. Everything was cold and dripping wet.

April's cries became more pitiful as she shook from the gathering chill. Marylee stretched out her baggy sweater and held April against her stomach, with the sweater and her coat wrapped around both of them, their skin pressed together, sharing warmth.

She sat unmoving in the dark, her back against the cold wall, willing her warmth to enter April's tiny body and stop the violent shivering. At last it stopped, and Marylee could tell by the sudden weight against her that the baby had fallen asleep, despite the shuddering sobs that shook her every few minutes.

During all this time, she had barely been aware of Petey's actions. She could hear him moving around inside the station, talking gently, sorrowfully to Camper. She could hear, too, the panting sounds made by the old dog, punctuated by low whimpering.

"We've got to have warmth," Petey said suddenly in the dark. "I – I can't stop Camper's shivering. There's an old wood stove in the corner. The burner things are gone, but I think it'll work. I've got some matches, but I'm going to have to find something to burn."

Marylee nodded, forgetting he couldn't see her.

"You'll look after Camper, won't you?" Petey asked, his voice sounding young and frightened. "I'll be real quick, but I think he's sick. You'll look after him?"

"I'll look after him," Marylee promised. "Camper's a great old dog, so – I'll look after him."

Petey hesitated a second or two longer, then quickly pulled himself through the hole in the boards.

He seemed to be gone a long time, but with nothing to do but care for April and Camper, Marylee couldn't be sure. Once when Camper was whimpering, she carefully leaned over and stroked his head. She could feel the damp material of Petey's jacket and shirt over the dog's back. Under her fingers, she could feel him shivering.

"Take it easy, fellow," she murmured softly. "Petey'll be back soon and then we'll feed you and get you warmed up."

Camper whimpered slightly and licked her fingers. Marylee hesitated a moment, then carefully put her own jacket over the dog as well. Her arms felt the chill of the cold air instantly, but April would be kept warm by her body.

Twice Marylee felt a warm trickle of water running down her stomach as April urinated in her sleep. She hunched over in revulsion, but there was no way of preventing it and still keeping her baby warm. And she must care for her child.

She heard several thuds on the floor beside her, under the hole. Then Petey climbed in through the opening and crouched down beside her.

"Is Camper okay?" he asked anxiously.

"I'm not sure. I guess so," Marylee answered. The dog was still shivering and panting in the chill, dank air.

Petey struck a match, and in the brief flare of light Marylee saw that his hair was plastered to his head and the water was running down his face and bare back. Camper was lying on his side, mouth open, eyes half shut, sides heaving under the pile of clothes they had put over him.

Quickly Petey laid a fire inside the gaping stove. He used several matches before the soggy paper and wood scraps he'd found would light, and even after the flame caught, the fire smoked and sputtered, threatening every minute to go out. But there was a little heat radiating from it.

First spreading out his jacket for the old dog to lie on, Petey carefully moved Camper closer to the heat. When he had the dog lying as close to the stove as he dared, he laid his shirt and Marylee's jacket over him again.

"We'll need more wood," he muttered to Marylee.

She nodded, and again he hoisted himself out of the break in the wood. It didn't seem as long this time before he returned. There were several loud thumps as he dropped a large armful of kindling into the garage. After three more series of thumps, each about ten minutes apart, he crawled back into the station.

"I found a house a ways back on the road with a huge pile of firewood," he said with satisfaction as he crouched beside Camper again. "It's dry, and they had so much they'll never miss what I took."

"That's great," Marylee said quietly, but with little conviction. Everything's working out fine, she told herself – you're just tired. Just tired.

For a long time she sat without saying anything more, trying to keep her mind away from the dragging depression that was settling over her. She watched Petey crouch over his dog, talking to him, petting him, trying to get him to swallow a dog biscuit he had mixed with some of the milk they had brought for April.

Camper thumped his tail slightly, but the food Petey so gently placed in his mouth just dribbled out again. Twice, in the dim light of the fire, Marylee could see tears slipping from Petey's eyes. He didn't try to hide them and she said nothing. Through the numbness that had possessed her, Marylee felt his sorrow and fear and joined in it.

All the fierce joy and the wild emotions seemed gone from her now, carried away by the cold and the dark and the rain. Her love for the baby was still deep within her, but the bland contentment she had experienced in the warehouse was gone. With numb detachment, she sensed it would be gone forever. It was as if the world had suddenly become real to her again. Because of April, this reality was not so cold and hating as before, but it was as implacable as it had always been.

As the child stirred against her, a gentle smile flickered across Marylee's face. She watched Petey sitting, grieving beside Camper, and somehow she felt all the love he had for his dog. It was a mirror of the love she felt for April – a love of needing and giving. A giving of everything.

Then, unable to hold it away any longer, Marylee remembered the face of April's real mother pleading for her child – the terrible pain and the grief. Mixed with the woman's agony, she remembered the fluttering pink gingham and the gurgling laugh that would well up from April's round stomach. She remembered the hours of fear and frustration as she paced back and forth in the grey warehouse while April screamed and twisted, and the soft sighs that slipped from the baby as she nestled her head into Marylee's shoulder.

Then, as the dawn light began to filter into the dirty corners of the garage, she tried to see the future as it must be. Because of her numb exhaustion, Marylee was able to see it without the daydreams of smiles and games with April, surrounded by frills and flowers and warm breezes.

Petey could do no more for them, she sensed. Instead of the dreams, she saw what must be the reality – the grinding fear of being found with a baby the world said did not belong to her; the cold and the desperation as she tried to find a place where she and April could live, and money just to buy the food they needed.

It occurred to her that she could manage somehow...somehow. But what would that do to April? What would that kind of life do to her child?

An hour after sunrise, Petey stood up and lifted Camper into his arms. "I'm going," he told Marylee. His face was grimy, streaked with tears.

She stared at him a moment, the old words of anger and manipulation already forming in her mouth, then April whimpered and butted her head against her stomach.

"If I don't find a vet...I..I think he'll die." Petey's voice stuttered his fear.

The numbness suddenly seeped away from Marylee's mind and she realized she couldn't do it again. She rose to her feet, and gently pulled Camper's ear.

"It's time to go home," she said slowly.

Chapter Nine

Truth

The air was summer warm and the sunlight flickered on the wings of the butterflies and insects as Marylee and Petey trudged back toward the town. After the hard silence that had existed between them for so long, they chattered and giggled for much of the time, only occasionally falling into deep, aching silence.

They sat for a few minutes at the edge of a park, while Marylee gave April the last bottle of milk. Camper suddenly scrambled from Petey's arms, walked a few feet and relieved himself. When it was time to move on, Petey picked him up again. The dog licked his chin and April laughed and waved her arms.

At the outskirts of the town they dropped their last dime into the coin slot and took out a local paper. The story of April's kidnapping had been reduced to just a small item as other events claimed the newspaper's attention.

But the article mentioned that the search was being conducted from the family's home at 83 Weaver Place.

"That's about five blocks from here," Petey said quietly. "That way. It's probably one of those big fancy places we passed yesterday."

When they turned the corner to Weaver Place, Petey and Marylee saw a police car parked in front of the house. There were other cars as well, but no one noticed the two weary children carrying an old dog, or even the baby, as they trudged grimly down the street. A boy on a bicycle turned his eyes away in unconscious revulsion when he noticed Marylee's heavy limp. April gurgled to herself and tried to stick her fingers between Marylee's clenched teeth.

When they reached the house, Petey sat down on the grassy curb, hugging Camper, and stared silently at the police car parked on the opposite side of the road. Marylee hesitated a moment, then resolutely walked up to the heavy brown front door and fiercely banged the wrought iron knocker.

The door opened wide and a woman Marylee recognized stood in front of her.

She should have been pretty, but her face was white and swollen. Her eyes were glazed with exhaustion, and her dark hair hung limp.

With a searing agony, Marylee noticed it was the same color as April's.

"Oh, my God!" the woman cried hoarsely as she stared at Marylee and April. Joy and relief surged across her face as she took her baby from the girl.

"I've brought April – Jo – JoAnne back to you," Marylee said numbly. She thought she would die. If only she could die right now.

People began to surge around them, and April looked uncertainly at her two mothers, her lip quivering in confusion. The woman clutched her daughter to her, crying and repeating her name, over and over.

Marylee stood numb and staring, ignoring the people who were asking her loud questions.

"Will you let me see her once in a while?" she asked suddenly.

"See her?" Mrs. Massey repeated, dazed, holding the baby tightly.

"Yes," Marylee said, her voice curiously hollow. "I didn't really kidnap her – we thought she had been abandoned. I was abandoned.... She's so beautiful, I couldn't stand the idea of no one ever wanting her. You see, I wanted her. She has been my baby. I've been her mother, and I love her so much. I love her...."

Her voice trailed off as she stared at her baby – the other woman's baby.

Jean Massey looked at the plain, crippled girl, and with senses heightened from weeks of fear, saw the white agony passing over her face. This girl loved JoAnne almost as much – no, she realized with a shock, as much as she did.

They were alone, the two mothers, isolated from the jubilant, questioning strangers who milled around them.

"I wouldn't have brought her back," Marylee said defiantly. "I would have kept her, because I'm a good mother. I love her so much – so much. But I couldn't look after her right. It was hard to find a place to live. We stayed in an empty warehouse, but that would be too cold for winter. And Petey got caught shoplifting, trying to get food and blankets for her. We had no money. No money at all and nowhere to go. I love April too much to let her grow up like me – someone with nowhere to go."

Marylee closed her eyes for a moment.

When she opened them again, April – JoAnne – was in the arms of her father. Voices were laughing and shouting around them, but her baby's mother was looking at her still, with sadness-darkened eyes.

Jean Massey watched the stiff, limping figure go down the walk and away from the house. "Where is Solomon when you need him?" she murmured.

Afternoon sunlight was flooding into the warehouse again, making Marylee's shadow stream across the floor. She hugged her legs to herself and tried to remember the bits of poetry:

Aspens shiver, red maples wave
While I and my enemies – friends – lie
Still
In the grave...

Her whispers trailed off.

Stupid poem, she muttered to herself as she got up, cautiously flexing her numbed toes, waiting for the pins-and-needles feeling of circulation to begin.

A week had passed, long and agonizing. People had asked questions constantly – police, reporters, social workers, the Watsons, everyone. But Marylee had remained silent. Sometimes the voices barely even pierced the quiet agony she was living in.

As often as she could, Marylee had slipped away to walk hesitantly by the house where her baby now lived, hoping she would see her through a window, or perhaps outside sunning. Once she almost knocked on the door, but at the last minute had decided she could not bear to talk to the Masseys again.

She never had a glimpse of her baby.

Today she had come to the warehouse hoping to find peace, and perhaps a few things left behind that were April's. Tomorrow she would be removed to the Residential Children's Treatment Center on the other side of town. She wouldn't have another chance to visit the warehouse.

Petey had said he would water her garden, but they both knew he would never come near the warehouse again, despite his promise. Marylee doubted that she would even see him again. Everything had changed for Petey.

The numbness had left her foot, so Marylee limped over to the window for one last look at her garden. Maybe Petey – ? But no, she told herself. Petey would not come back now.

The summer sun had been streaming through the green curtained windows when Marylee limped into the family court that morning with Mrs. Wojansky. The store that Petey had taken the baby things from was pressing charges against him, as they had said they would.

"I'll wait in the hall," Mrs. Wojansky murmured in Marylee's ear.

Wordlessly Marylee nodded, then entered the courtroom and limped to a seat midway down the aisle. She stared around. At the front she saw Petey, looking strangely scrubbed and tidied, shifting nervously in his chair. A blonde woman and a big man sat on either side of him – his mother and Mike. A few official looking men and women moved slowly about the room, making subdued noises. Marylee heard the door to the court creak open behind her, but didn't bother to see who had come in.

In a few minutes everyone stood up as the judge entered, and soon the heating got underway. Petey was told to go stand near the bench.

"Do you understand why we're having this hearing, Peter?" the judge asked austerely, peering over her glasses at Petey.

"Yes, ma'am," Petey mumbled almost inaudibly, unconsciously rubbing the palms of his hands on the front of his slacks.

"And what do you think about it?"

Petey shrugged unsurely.

The judge shuffled some papers on the table in front of her.

"The reports we have about you say that

this is the first time you've been in trouble with the law, but that you are considered a troublemaker at school. Is that true?"

"I guess so," Petey mumbled.

"Mrs. Davies, would you approach the bench, please?"

Petey's mother glanced nervously at Mike, then walked up to stand beside her son.

"You work at the telephone company as a night time customer service rep, is that correct?" the judge asked.

"Yes, ma'am. I've worked there for almost ten years."

"While you're working, who cares for your son?"

"Well, up until a couple of years ago one of our neighbors would put him to bed and keep an eye on him. But she's moved away now, and Petey's always been pretty self-reliant. I mean, he didn't seem to need anybody, and he's never been in trouble before."

"I see," said the judge. She sighed. Why couldn't people be bothered to look after their children?

"The circumstances surrounding this theft are a little unusual, I understand," she went on. "Is Marylee Jones here?"

Marylee stood up self-consciously.

"Good. Come up here to the bench, please,

and explain what you believe led up to this unfortunate incident."

Slowly Marylee limped to the front of the courtroom.

It began hammering in Marylee's mind that this wasn't right, that it wasn't Petey's fault. It was her fault. She had to make the judge see that it was her fault. He had to understand about April. About how desperate they were. About how Petey was a good father....

She began talking slowly, saying the words that had hovered for so long in her mind, pouring out the emotions that had simmered in her stomach. Vaguely, she realized that she strayed often from what strictly concerned Petey, but no one interrupted her. The court held the atmosphere of truth, and it was the time for Marylee's truth.

Then there was silence for a time. Marylee felt clean, the way she had that summer long ago when she had emptied her hate into the rushing water. The sun now streaming through the windows was the same summer sun that had warmed her and healed her once before. When she turned to limp back to her seat, she saw the man and woman to whom she had given her baby. She smiled slightly, and they smiled back, concern and warmth etched on their faces.

"Excuse me." Mike's deep voice addressed the judge, breaking the silence.

"I'm sorry to interrupt, ma'am," he continued, "but before you decide what should be done about Petey, I hope you'll take this into consideration. His mother and I are going to be married next week, and Doreen will be able to quit her night job and look for one with more regular hours. At any rate, once we're married Petey will have a normal home life – because that's really what he's needed – and I'll make sure he doesn't get into trouble like this again."

"No," Petey mumbled, unbelieving. "No!" He sprang to his feet. "We don't need you!" he shouted accusingly at Mike. "We don't want you! We did just fine before you came along. And I proved it! I proved I could live through it, Mom – like you told me. I lived through that kind of hell. I was a father for April – I really was – and I didn't take off. I didn't...." Petey's voice trailed off as the sobs shook his shoulders. He crossed his arms over his face so that no one could see his tears.

"Oh, Petey," his mother began softly.

"No, Doreen," Mike interrupted.

"Petey," he said firmly. Petey wiped his face on his sleeve, then met Mike's eyes fiercely. Mike calmly returned his stare.

"You're right, Petey," he said. "You did fine.

You know that you did what you had to, not just acting like a man – but as a man. But I'm a man too, and I love your mom. I'm not taking her away from you – I couldn't if I wanted to – but I'm going to be a part of your lives now, like it or not."

"You mean, I'm not losing a mother, I'm gaining a father," Petey sneered.

Mike's eyes met his.

"That's right, kid," he stated calmly.

Marylee held her breath. She knew it could work out. It could be a family. But Mike had done it wrong. She knew Petey. He'd shout obscenities, strike out....

There was a long, measuring silence. Then suddenly Marylee saw the edge of Petey's mouth quirk briefly into a slight smile. It was going to be all right.

Petey shrugged and slouched back into his chair. "Better watch your step then, or I'll throw you out," he murmured impudently.

Mike grinned, and touched Petey's shoulder lightly.

"I think we'll manage, sir," Mike told the judge.

The severe expression on the judge's face relaxed into a smile.

"Yes," she replied, "I think so too. On the basis of that, Petey, and the fact that your actions, although misguided, were responsibly motivated, I'm going to put you on a year's probation. And I don't want to see you in this court again."

The hearing ended with details Marylee didn't care about. She turned around in her seat, determined to ask about April, but the Masseys were gone.

She waited a moment to speak to Petey, but when his mother stared coldly at her, she turned instead and limped out to the hall where Mrs. Wojansky was waiting for her.

"The Masseys stopped to talk to me for a minute," Mrs. Wojansky murmured. "What nice people they seem to be. They seem very interested in you, Marylee."

Marylee looked at her, wondering what she meant, what had been said. But the woman said no more, so sadly she shoved it into the back of her mind.

Marylee stared out the window of the warehouse and thought about Petey. She ought to feel happy for him. She did feel happy for him, but it was hard to imagine what his life would be like now.

With certainty, she knew that her own days with even a semblance of a family were over. Mrs. Wojansky had told her yesterday that she was going to live in a center for "troubled" children – that they would try to help her there.

"Perhaps some day," she whispered to herself, "perhaps some day I'll have a family of my own. A little baby of my own...."

She stared down at the garden. The seeds had sprouted quickly. Leaves had branched out.

"Funny," she murmured to herself. "I didn't think the ground was good enough. It looked so barren. Another few days and there might be flowers too, if there was someone here to water them."

Again she stared out at the dirty stream and tried to imagine how things would be if life were perfect. April would be her baby, all hers. They would live in a big house together – one like the house her baby lived in now. And there would be a happy, laughing man to be her father.

But then, where would that leave Jean Massey, April's other mother?

"Nothing's any good," Marylee muttered to herself. She knew now that she would never inflict that hurt on the woman, even if she could.

For a moment Marylee thought of how it would be if she could live with the Masseys. If she could be their foster child – a mother's helper.

"I'd never interfere with the way they're bringing you up, April," she whispered. If only she could be near her baby.

She stared off down the stream, trying to clear the blur from her eyes. There were two figures walking along the bank – Mrs. Wojansky and a man.

Marylee watched them come closer and closer to the warehouse. They were talking cheerfully to each other, she noticed with little interest. Maybe he was the person in charge of the center.

Suddenly Marylee stiffened.

"Oh, no," she whispered. The man was April's father. But why was he coming to the warehouse with Mrs. Wojansky? Why were they coming to see her?

"Maybe they do want me to come live with them," she murmured, hardly daring to say the words. Her hands gripped the window ledge and her knuckles whitened. She remembered the agonized look in Jean Massey's face – the understanding in her dark eyes. Could she have just one dream come true?

They came closer.

"Oh, God," Marylee whispered once more. A strange calm seeped over her. "Oh, God, please let it be. Let me go to my baby."

Epilogue

Spring had turned to summer five times since the day the Masseys brought Marylee home. Even with therapy from the specialized treatment center, she had not been easy for the Masseys, for the stunted growth of a cold, bleak spring takes much time and love before blossoming into the warmth of summer.

Today she stood once again in front of the warehouse – an almost unwilling pilgrim, pulled back by the hard and beautiful memories that gave her a path to healing. As she stared at the barren ugliness of the warehouse, the hard, grey lines softened in her thoughts, and the emptiness was peopled again by the joy that began there.

JoAnne (she rarely called her April now) was almost six, and was as beautiful and joyful as only love can make a child. Her springs had been full of warmth and caring, and she blossomed.

Now, as Marylee stood at the edge of another summer, all the early, cold promises she lived had changed. For as surely as spring merges into summer, she knew that because she had once learned to love in this place, she would love and be loved – again and again.

And now a Sneak Peek at

Sammy and the Devil Dog

Everything has gone wrong in Sammy's life. She's in constant trouble at school and the local bully won't leave her alone. When Sammy rescues an abused dog named Jack, her problems get even worse. Jack never learned to be a good dog – he's wild and unpredictable. How can Sammy teach him how much they need each other?

Hey, Chicken Man!

A new edition of this best-selling book!
Tom Kirby is chicken and everybody knows it. Billy MacPherson has made sure of that.

Hidden in the thick woods of the Niagara Escarpment, the gang of boys has gathered for the final initiation. Any moment now, the runoff will come gushing through the Tunnel – and Andrew will be drowned!

"You save him! He's your friend," Billy taunts.

Blindly Tom runs into the Tunnel, fighting back his terror as the cold blackness closes around him...

Hey, Chicken Man!

by

Susan Brown

Chapter One

Chicken Man

Tom Kirby was chicken and everybody knew it. Billy MacPherson had made sure of that.

From where he lay in the shade of the cherry tree, Tom could see Billy and the others strung out in a dusty line of bicycles on the road that bounded the orchard. Probably Billy had decided that the gang would head towards the conservation area for a swim.

Tom's stomach seized up. He wanted to disappear, to sink deeply into the shorn grass of his family's orchard before the boys got close enough to see him. But he was too proud to move.

Billy had almost passed by before he noticed Tom lying motionless in the shade of the small tree. Their eyes met for an instant, then Billy wheeled his bicycle around and stared with raised eyebrows.

"Well!" he said in mock surprise as the others pulled up around him. "Look who we have here!"

"Chicken Man!" Skinner drawled in his high, nasal voice.

Tom was used to this, but he winced inwardly when Chris, Joey and Mike chanted in much-practiced unison, "Buck-cluck-cluck!"

He stared into the distance with as little expression on his face as he could manage while they roared and snickered.

"Well, c'mon, Cobras," Billy said with exaggerated contempt. "We have better things to do than cackle with Chicken Man."

The others snickered again and rode off down the road shouting, "See ya, Chicky!" And "Look out for the Cobras!" behind them.

Tom lay unmoving until he was sure they were out of sight. Then he jumped up and threw down the grass stem he had been chewing. He stared in the direction they had gone and clenched his fists. For a moment he thought about how good it would feel to smash Billy MacPherson a good one right in his fat, leering face. But that wouldn't help. The others would still yell "Chicken!" at him when they knew they were out of range.

Tom strode off towards the other side of the orchard. He yanked his bike out of the shed and set off down the lane and onto the gravel side road. He paused for a minute and thought of going to swim at the conservation area despite Billy, then decided against it. There was no point in asking for punishment.

They'd never jump him, of course. Billy was a bully, not a fool. They'd tried that once last fall, but Tom had just fought it out as best he could, landing a few good punches and taking about three dozen. But the next day he had waited until he could get Billy by himself and had blacked his eye and given him a nosebleed. For all his size and bullying, Billy was no fighter without the others to back him up.

As the tires of Tom's bicycle scrunched over the gravel, the dry dust of the side road billowed around him. He pumped hard up the steep, curved hill that led into town. After the first fifteen meters, the hill was less steep, but it continued with a slight incline for about one and a half kilometers until it reached the town. Then there was a sharp curve and another steep section as the road snaked up the side of the Niagara Escarpment.

Tom was perspiring heavily and his face was streaked with dust by the time he reached town. He thought of riding to a fast food place for a coke, then changed his mind. He didn't feel like seeing anyone this morning. With a sudden fierce need to get entirely away from people, he began the hard ride up the road leading to the top of the Escarpment. He managed to pedal about seventy-five meters up the steep road past town before he had to get off and walk. It gave him a sense of satisfaction.

At the top of the road, Tom stopped to rest at the gravel turn-off the government had built for sightseers. He loved the view more than any other in the area.

Leaning on his bicycle, he could survey almost every bit of the countryside he knew so well. There at his feet was the Escarpment, covered with brush and trees and patches of bare rock where the incline was too sharp for even the tough bushes to find a secure hold. In front lay the prairie-like flatness of – what? A valley maybe? But there were no hills on the other side, just the glittering, blue expanse of Lake Ontario stretching to the horizon.

Tom often wondered what had made the land so flat. He felt as though he could almost reach out and run his hand over the rich textures of the countryside, like some huge possessive giant: the patches of green orchards like mossy velvet, the vineyards like spikey grass terracing, the buildings like scattered building blocks, and the Queen Elizabeth Way, stretching south and east to Niagara Falls, like a ribbon of hard glue, sun-dried in a random pattern.

From where he stood he could see a familiar cluster of houses. His own home stood out, bright white and sprawling, with its pinkish, pointed and partly gabled roof. His parents had bought it because it was so old – almost a hundred and fifty years. Surrounding it were the two small orchards, one of cherries, the other of peaches. The big white shed that served as a garage and catch-all was actually an old carriage house from before the days of cars.

The other houses seemed more naked than his own because they were new structures, unscreened by trees, less belonging to the area. Just over a year ago Billy MacPherson's parents had bought the big, showy one at the far end.

Tom's teeth clenched as he thought of Billy again. If it hadn't been for Billy, no one would ever have thought of the initiation and he would still be the one who decided things, instead of Billy. No one but Billy could have found Tom's own private weakness, the one he'd never told anyone. Until Billy came along, it had just been a rough edge on the back of his mind, something that grated sometimes but was usually easy to avoid and forget.

Abruptly Tom turned his back on the view. He'd show them. He'd go finish the initiation now. There was no time limit. He'd do it right now.

With cold determination, he pushed off on his bicycle. As he pedalled, Tom made plans about how he would casually flaunt the pocket-knife he would retrieve. He wouldn't come running up to Billy and the others the way Skinner had, shouting, "Look, I did it! I'm part of the gang now too, aren't I?"

No, Skinner was two years younger, and that was the way a little kid would do it. Tom would carry the knife in his back pocket, with maybe a small piece of wood. The next time Billy and the Cobras started to call him Chicken Man, he'd casually take the knife out and start to whittle. It would be rusty now from lying in the water for almost ten months but the orange rust would just add to the effect.

Tom gloated over his image of Billy's reaction. It would be worth all the humiliation of the past year to make a public fool out of Billy.

He forced his mind to dwell on the scene. If he allowed himself to think of what he had to do first, his stomach would seize up as it had so many other times, and the thought of the Black Tunnel would fill him with a terrible fear. No, he would just think of how he would make a fool of Billy.

I have to do it this time, he thought desperately. *This time has to be different.*

After a kilometer of furious pedalling, Tom was panting from the exertion. It was a long way. The trees had thinned, and for the rest of the way the road was exposed to the hot sun. The pavement ahead looked rippled, distorted by the rising heat waves.

Tom felt calmer now. At least if he didn't make it this time no one would know the difference. He would pretend he thought the whole thing was kid stuff and that he had no intention of ever trying it. They didn't have to know about all the Saturdays and vacations he had spent up here. Once he had even come in winter, though he had nearly killed himself climbing down the icy cliff.

If they didn't know, then things couldn't get any worse except in his own mind, Tom thought gloomily. Even his parents had started talking about his lack of confidence, his slipping grades and his anti-social behaviour. They didn't know the truth, because it wasn't the kind of thing that parents understand.

They thought he didn't want to hang around with the other kids, or play hockey, or anything. How could they know that the other kids would have nothing to do with him?

Tom continued slowly. Occasionally a car passed him, full of tourists taking the scenic route along the top of the Escarpment. This road was pretty but the one at the foot of the Escarpment was faster, so there weren't too many cars to spoil the quiet isolation of the morning.

Finally, Tom came to the old mill and stopped. It was now a museum, managed by the man whose great-grandfather had built the mill. Mr. Piers couldn't stand kids hanging around. Tom thought it was really funny how the old man would hover over the kids as though he were afraid they would break things. How could anyone break the insides of a mill made of wooden beams and iron? Or better still, how could anyone break a waterfall? Old Mr. Piers had even fenced that off.

Tom saw Mr. Piers poking around the grounds, pulling up the odd weed and nervously watching two boys who were innocently fishing in the widened river below the falls. He chuckled at the old man's frantic worry about what they might do.

Mr. Piers knew everything about the river that had once run the mill. He even made it his business to know what the people at the nearby waterworks plant were doing, because the runoff from the reservoir that supplied the town of Orchard Falls with water was occasionally released through man-made tunnels into the river's gorge.

There was a whole series of runoff tunnels in the Escarpment, Mr. Piers had once told Tom. They were interconnected, and some were several kilometers long, drilled through the solid, sweating limestone of the Escarpment. The Black Tunnel was one of these.

Tom got back on his bicycle and pedalled slowly down the road. When he was sure Mr. Piers wasn't watching, he swiftly turned into the rutted lane that led down behind the mill, past an abandoned farmhouse, into an overgrown field, and to the path that would take him down into the gorge.

He hid his bike in the bushes and began the difficult climb. Unless you looked carefully, the first section seemed impossibly steep until the cliff finally jumbled itself into a half-overgrown hill that angled down to the river.

But if you knew where to look and how to climb, here and there you could find a bit of rock where you could wedge your feet or find a handhold. There was one two-meter drop with no handholds. But at the side of it, a wild grape vine had spilled over the top of the cliff and sent its roots and seedlings into little cracks and crevices in the face of the rock until vines coated half the cliff face. The main vine, if you groped for it among all the leaves and tendrils of its offshoots, was about half as thick as a man's wrist. The boys had tested it three summers before and it had held the weight of five of them without budging.

Carefully Tom slid down on the seat of his jeans, until the cliff was too steep to go any farther that way. Then with a practiced movement he twisted over, hanging for support on a handy tree root that looped out of the rock. His feet scrabbled for a hold and finally found a thin outcropping. He wedged his other foot against a stone covered with sticky mud.

Carefully testing each foothold and handhold to see if it would bear his weight, Tom climbed down to where the cliff became too sheer to find any hold at all. Then he groped until he found the father vine. Once he had it grasped firmly in both hands, he pushed his feet free and with a Tarzan yell swung himself down the rest of the way. That was the best part of the climb. The scrapes and bruises were just the scars of a successful battle with the cliff.

Tom jumped and bounded the rest of the way down to the edge of the river. For a while he stood quietly in the complete isolation of the gorge. It was full of sounds – water sounds, bird sounds, wind sounds, even chipmunk, squirrel and other small animal sounds – but it seemed wonderfully still, because there were no people or machine noises. Down here, enclosed by the sheer sides of the gorge, even his cell phone couldn't pick up a signal.

With a surge of his old confidence, Tom walked slowly along the riverbank towards the roar of the waterfall. He hopped over rivulets that trickled from the sweating cliff into the river and jumped onto the cushioning softness of logs that had lain moist and unmoving for years, slowly rotting back into the ground.

He always felt that this was his own place, made especially for him. Adults never came here. The beauty of the gorge and the stream, with its progressively smaller waterfalls, was not enough to bring them clambering down the rough cliff. The tunnels that fed into the gorge had been blasted and mined out almost seventy-five years earlier. Tom wasn't sure if anyone besides him and Mr. Piers remembered they were there.

There were two tunnels opening into this part of the gorge. The smaller was high in the sheer cliff – a scar drilled into the rock of the Escarpment. It was impossible to climb to.

Farther up the gorge, the second tunnel was cut into the cliff beside the cool, bowl-shaped basin of the waterfall. A steep hill of loose rock and shale, refuse from when the tunnels had been drilled, spilled from the tunnel mouth, making it easy to reach.

There were few traces that the tunnels were not natural – only the rusted rails for the cars that had carried out the drilled rock, and the remains of a metal grille that had once been fastened over the entrance of the second tunnel to keep people and animals out of the drainage system. The grille had long ago been wrenched off, and now it lay with the rails in the water that covered the bottom of the tunnel.

Tom stared at the smaller tunnel. Directly in front of it was a semi-circular ledge about a meter wide, which narrowed down to nothing a couple of meters on either side of the tunnel. The spill-off of water had gouged a small pool in the ledge. Tom could see the rippling reflections of the water on the rock above the tunnel mouth. His pocket-knife was in that pool now, probably rusted and useless, a symbol of his own lack of courage.

To pass the initiation Tom had to retrieve the knife from the pool, and to do that he would have to enter the Black Tunnel. He'd have to stumble and grope his way through half a kilometer of cold, dripping darkness to the branching smaller tunnel, penetrating the very heart of the Escarpment. There was no other way to the pool.

Turning his back on the cliff, he strode angrily towards the waterfall. Well, he was going now to get that useless, rusted jack-knife. He would finish the initiation and overcome all his nightmare terrors.

He heard the roar of the waterfall as he clambered up the steep, gravelly hill. He didn't look up because he knew the cold, black mocking mouth of the Tunnel would be there, silent and unmoving.

It would always be there, waiting for him. Like a great evil, crouching beast it would be waiting for him to walk into its yawning, sweating mouth. And he *would* walk into its mouth – into the stony darkness that in his fears went on for a crushing eternity.

He stood before the indifferent, gaping blackness. There was no change in it since the last time. There never would be a change. The icy draft of air issuing from the depths of the Escarpment; the scarred, sweating rocks; the old grille submerged in the cold water, bit by bit rusting away – it was all the same.

Steadily Tom faced the Tunnel, daring himself to walk into its blackness and retrieve the useless, rusty jack-knife.

Sammy and the Devil Dog

by

Susan Brown

Chapter One

Let's See You Dance!

Sammy sat motionless, or as near to motionless as it was possible for her. Her eyes hardly left the house phone sitting on the kitchen counter. Eleven minutes before her mom came home. If the call didn't come before then, Sammy was dead...or maybe worse than dead.

Impatiently Sammy shoved her bangs out of her eyes. The movement made the bruise on her shoulder ache a little more, but she didn't care. She glanced at the clock. Nine minutes. Maybe the traffic would be bad. Maybe her mom would be delayed. Mrs. Martinez didn't have her mom's cell phone number, so the call would come here. Maybe this time Sammy would be lucky.

Lucky...not likely...

Six minutes.

Then, shattering the silence, the phone rang. Holding her breath, Sammy waited, counting the rings...*one...two...three...four....*

The answering machine picked up. *"Hi there. Sammy and Linda are dying to talk to you, but we aren't here! Leave a message. Leave a number. We'll call back!"*

"Hello, this is Tony from the Take a Stand Foundation. We're calling today..."

Sammy grabbed the receiver, held it at arms length for about three seconds and then slammed it down again. Silence. She looked at the clock.

Four minutes. Sammy drummed her fingers on the side of the table, and then lifted her head like a dog catching a distant sound.

"Oh no," she whispered. The painful rumble of her mom's old car turned into the long gravel drive.

"Oh, dirty dog, call now," she whispered, "Mrs. Martinez, call now...call now..."

The phone rang. *One...two...three...four...*

"Hi there. Sammy and Linda are dying to talk to you, but we aren't here! Leave a message. Leave a number. We'll call back!"

The rumbling engine suddenly stopped. The car door squealed open...

"Hello Ms. Connor. This is Jeanne Martinez, principal at Samantha's school. I'm afraid that Samantha was involved in another incident today. I'd like to schedule a meeting with you and your daughter to see what we can do to

help Samantha improve her behavior. I know there have been a lot of changes in your lives recently, but we can't allow her to continue to make such inappropriate choices. Please call me to schedule a time."

The message machine beeped. Sammy jabbed the erase button as Linda Connor pushed open the kitchen door.

"Hi Sammy, how was school?" her mom asked. "Can you help me with these bags? I can't believe how much I saved at the consignment store. I found the cutest top! I told you I had a date Saturday with a guy I met at the pottery sale, didn't I?"

When Sammy took the largest bag, her mom pulled a bright pink blouse from the other stuffed plastic bag and held it up to her chin. "What do you think?"

"It's great, mom," Sammy said. "Really a good color on you."

Her mom grinned. "Thanks, kiddo. I'm going to get cleaned up and get some work done in my studio. What are you up to?"

"Erin got back from Japan on Tuesday, so we're going to hang out," Sammy said. "Is that okay?"

Her mom was already pulling off her outer clothes before heading to the shower, but she stopped and gave Sammy a squeeze. "I'm really glad she's back. This has been a tough time for you to be by yourself, without your best friend."

Sammy hugged back. "You too."

Her mom laughed a little shakily, and ran her fingers through her hair. "That's life," she said. "It just keeps on happening whether you're ready or not. I need to get cleaned up."

Sammy smiled like the good kid she used to be, until her mom was out of sight. Then she took the house phone off its cradle, turned it on, and dropped it to the floor. In a smooth motion, she nudged it behind and under the counter.

"And stay there," Sammy said.

Problem dealt with, Sammy ran out back to get her bike. She and Erin were meeting at the convenience store. When Sammy had puffed her way up the long hill, Erin was waiting for her outside the store with two big freezies in her hands. When she tried to wave with the cups in her hand, it looked so funny, Sammy started to laugh.

Jumping off, Sammy propped her bike against the wall and took a long frozen slurp, so cold it almost burned. "Oh," she sighed blissfully, "you will be my best friend forever."

Erin giggled, took a long slurp herself, and then looked at her seriously.

172   Susan Brown

"Did your mom understand that you couldn't help that fight?" she demanded. "That the girls were making that little kid cry by teasing him?"

"Sure," Sammy said jerking the straw up and down. "My mom's great that way."

Erin frowned. "She didn't used to be," she said slowly. "You used to always go to your grandpa."

"Well," Sammy's voice had a weird scratch to it, "he's not here so I guess she just picked it up instead."

"Oh Sammy," Erin cried. "I am such a bad friend. I am so sorry. I shouldn't have said anything. Don't be sad!"

Her eyes held such pleading that Sammy forced herself to laugh. "It's okay," she said. "Come on – let's ride somewhere."

"Your house," Erin said. "I haven't seen it."

"Yes, you have," Sammy said.

"But not when you lived there," Erin said earnestly. "I'll bet it's entirely different now. And special because you're there."

"You're going to be disappointed," Sammy said, getting back on her bike. She didn't want to go home, but then she thought of the phone under the cupboard. Her mom would be out of the shower by now, and might notice it wasn't there. And Sammy really wanted to stay out of trouble for awhile. Last week her mom had been so mad when Sammy got blamed for wrecking the class field trip – she just hadn't realized everyone had already gotten on the bus.

Glumly, Sammy leaned back on the bike, pushed off and slowly coasted away from the store letting gravity do all the work while she sipped her drink and lightly steered with one hand.

Aaw-oooo-oooo.

Sammy must have imagined the noise – it didn't belong in the trim suburb by the convenience store.

Aaw-oooo-oooo. A dog howl, mournful and low. Alone. Lonely.

Sammy jerked her head around, nearly lost her balance and just in time, swerved out of the way of a car. Her freezie spun across the road in a fizzing whirl.

Honk! The woman glared as she sped past.

"You don't own the road!" Sammy shouted. She smacked her hands on the handlebars. Erin, completely unaware, coasted down the hill.

Aaw-oooo-oooo.

Weird. This was weird. Sammy pushed back her helmet, trying to hear better. Animal cries, whimpering. And then....

Bang! Bang! Bang! Bangbangbang!

A dog yelped and cried. Laughter exploded through the air.

Sammy dropped her bike on the grass curb. The noises came from the yard that backed onto the sidewalk. A chain link fence, thick with vines, blocked her view.

The dog's cry rose again then trailed away.

Without hesitating, Sammy toe-climbed to the top of the fence. In a weedy back yard, two teenage boys were laughing so hard they could hardly stand up. A black dog, long-legged and shaggy, was nearly strangling himself trying to escape the chain that held him to a tree. A litter of red paper fluttered across the beaten dirt. The smell of gunpowder snagged Sammy's nostrils.

"Hey, dummy!" the tallest boy yelled to the dog. "Let's see you dance."

He held up a string of red firecrackers, struck a match, and lit the fuse. He boy threw them at the dog. The animal whimpered, leaped frantically into the air, then fell heavily as the chain nearly choked him. The crackers hissed and sputtered near his face.

"Stop!" Sammy screamed.

She leapt down from the fence and raced across the yard. The fuse was almost gone when Sammy kicked.

The first cracker went off as her toe hit the pack. She felt the smack and heard the pop. But the rest of the string flew in smooth arc back toward the boys.

"Hey!" they howled as the firecrackers popped and banged at their feet.

"How do you like dancing!" Sammy tore over to them. Firecrackers, big ones, were going off in her brain. "How could you do that? You are wicked and cruel and you deserve to die!"

"Ah shut up, you little witch!" the shorter boy snarled.

The biggest one leaned against the wall though and grinned. "We weren't hurting it. But that was a good move, kid. Real good kick."

"Get off our property!" The first one glared.

"Not a chance!" Sammy jabbed her fists into her hips. "I'm going to call the police and they're going to arrest you for cruelty to animals. You were torturing that dog!"

"What torture," the tallest teenager demanded. "We're training our dog to be a watchdog. And a watchdog is no good unless it's mean."

"You're just hurting it. You can't do that!"

"Yes we can – it's our dog."

Sammy narrowed her eyes and tried to decide if she had any chance of survival if she smacked that superior grin right off his face. What would Papa Jack have done?

"Sammy?" Erin was hanging onto the fence, peering over the top. "What's going on? Are you okay?"

"Yes, but those jerks were throwing fire crackers at him." Sammy turned to the animal. The dog was trying to hide behind the tree, pulling on his chain, making soft yelping noises. "Oh, you poor thing..."

She walked slowly toward it, holding out her hand. "He's just a puppy!" At the sound of her voice, the dog swiveled so that it crouched, nose pointing toward her.

"Oh you beautiful thing," Sammy crooned. The sun shone on the dog's rich black coat and gleamed on the long white diamond on his forehead. His two front paws and the thick ruff on his chest were clean white too. Sammy crouched and held out her hand. The dog sprang at her.

Sammy leaped back, tripped and fell. The dog stood over her, snarling. Black eyes ringed with white; black lips curled above white fangs. Sammy couldn't move, didn't dare move.

And then another boy ran past, grabbed the dog's chain and hauled him off. The dog barked and snapped.

"Shut up!" The boy smacked the dog on the head. The dog whimpered again and dropped down, head on its too-big puppy paws. The wild black eyes warmed to brown. The edge of a soft pink tongue peeked between its lips.

Sammy sat up. "Brian? Brian Haydon? What are you doing here?"

"I live here, stupid."

Sammy scrambled to her feet. "Here? I thought you lived in the apartments."

Brian shrugged. "We moved. That's why I got a dog. But he isn't any good."

Sammy took a deep breath, making the world look normal again. The pup's white-tipped tail thumped once.

"Do you know what they were doing to him?" Sammy demanded.

Brian looked up at the teenagers leaning against the wall. His face got hard. "Joe, I'm training the dog. You probably ruined him."

"Aah, what a shame," the big one, Joe, said. "You're such a woos, Brian. Besides we didn't hurt him – much. Cm'on Kyle. Play you, *Die Again Sucka*, on the computer."

They banged into the house. Brian swore under his breath.

"Who are *they*?" Erin hopped down from the fence, careful to keep a long way from the dog. She pushed her helmet more securely onto her dark hair.

"My brothers." Brian's voice had a snarl in it, kind of like the dog.

"It's against the law to abuse a dog," Erin told him. "You can't do that."

"I don't abuse him," Brian muttered.

"You just hit him on the head," Sammy retorted.

Brian scowled. "You have to be strict with a dog or he won't know who his master is."

"No! Not that strict," Sammy insisted.

She walked as close as she dared to the dog. He lifted his head and growled deep in his throat. "It's okay," she said softly. "Can't you tell I'm your friend?" The dog stared at her. His tail thumped again. He cocked his head.

"What kind of dog is he?" Sammy asked.

"Mutt," Brian said. "Got him from a guy down the street when he was a puppy."

The kids studied the dog who stared back at them. "I think he's part lab," Erin said. "He's black like a lab."

"He's too big," Brian scoffed.

"And his fur is too long," Sammy agreed. "And he has white on his chest."

The dog's head lifted a little more, and this time his tail really thumped.

She crouched down, flipped her hair from her eyes, and leaned toward the dog. "You want to be friendly, don't you boy?" She held out her hand, back first, fingers curled down.

The dog stood up. His tail straightened behind him.

"Good boy," she whispered.

Quicker than she could see, he leaped. She felt his hot breath, heard the snarl in his throat and glimpsed his sharp white teeth as they closed on her bare arm.

"No!" Sammy cried. "Bad dog!"

In the background she was aware of Erin shrieking. Furious, Sammy leaned closer to the dog's face. His teeth pressed painfully on her arm and his growl was low and steady.

"You let go," she said. "You be a good dog and let go."

She felt as though her eyes had a thin line of energy connecting directly to the dog's deep brown ones. The growl rumbled slowly. The jaws tightened a little, teeth not yet breaking the skin but soon...

"I'm not the bad guy," she whispered through gritted teeth. "I'm nice. You don't have to bite me and we can be friends. You need a friend."

The dog blinked, then suddenly yelped. Brian hauled him back roughly by the collar, and smacked him on the head again. The dog growled and bared his teeth.

"You stupid, no good dog," the boy berated him. "Drop it!" *Whack.* He smacked the dog again.

The dog backed up, lips curled and teeth gleaming in a deep snarl.

"Stop it!" Sammy yelled. "Don't you hit that dog again!"

Brian shook his head. "You got to be tough with a dog. Look how big and strong he is already. And he's only five months old. My Dad says he's a real devil. If I don't make him scared of me, what's going to make him do what I say?"

"Dogs do what you tell them because they love you!" Erin protested tearfully. "My golden retriever, Casey, does everything I tell her and she doesn't growl at me either. She loves me. She'd die for me."

Brian shrugged. "Jack was a real cute puppy. He slept with me until Dad said he had to be chained up out here and get turned into a watch dog."

Sammy thrust her chin forward. "If you hurt this dog again we'll report it to the police and you'll all get fined and go to jail."

Brian got a hard look on his face. "Ooh, I'm scared."

"I've warned you." Sammy headed to the fence, rubbing her arm. Bluish-purple tooth marks indented her skin and a line of pain crept past her elbow. The dog stared at her unblinking. "So long, boy," she said.

It took about two seconds to scramble over the fence. She rubbed her arm again. There was going to be a bruise but the dog hadn't broken the skin. He could have, couldn't he, if he wanted to? Maybe the dog didn't really want to hurt her.

"Do you think we should call the police?" Erin interrupted her thoughts.

"Maybe." Sammy picked up her bike from the grass. "Brian will beat us up at school."

"Oh, he wouldn't, because we're girls," Erin insisted.

"That's never stopped him before," Sammy said.

Brian was about six inches taller, twice as heavy and three times as strong as any other kid at Carr Elementary. When anyone, any age or size bugged him, he punched them out. Once, he'd shoved the PE teacher and pulled a five days suspension.

"Brian is disgusting – disgusting and weird." Erin tightened her helmet strap and pushed off, gliding smoothly down the bike lane.

Sammy looked back at the fence, wondering what the dog was doing now. What had Brian called him? She froze. *Jack!* The dog's name was Jack. Sammy bit her lip and pedaled slowly after her friend.

"How could Brian name his dog Jack?" she demanded.

ABOUT THE AUTHOR

Adventure, mystery, and magic propel Susan Brown, fuelling her imagination into writing more and more stories for kids and teens.

Susan lives with her two border collie rescue dogs amid wild woods and overgrown gardens in Snohomish, Washington. From there she supervises her three daughters, assorted sons-in-law and two grandsons. It's a great way to be a writer!

Free stories and news about upcoming books at:
www.susanbrownwrites.com

Susan is also one half of Stephanie Browning, the pen name shared with her writing partner of close to a thousand years, Anne Stephenson.
www.stephaniebrowningromance.com

Susan is a founding member of the Writers Cooperative of the Pacific Northwest, a group of independent writers working together to bring readers great books!
http://www.writers-coop.com

62268476R00109

Made in the USA
Lexington, KY
02 April 2017